# Hell No, We Won't Go

### A Novel by

## Jim Stevens

2014 by Jim Stevens

The final approval of this literary material is granted by the author.

First Printing

ISBN: 978-0-9849247-8-3

For NJS

## Prologue

"There is a tide in the affairs of men. Which, taken in the flood, leads on to fortune."

Forty years ago I would have been the last person on earth to quote Shakespeare, but a lot can change in forty years. It's been that long since I set foot on this campus. I haven't missed it, and seldom think about it. I've been invited back numerous times. People have found me, called me, offered to pay me to return, but I always refuse. I had no interest. The flood passed, and the fortunes I once believed were mine went out with the tide.

I return today, not for me, but for my father.

I park the rental car on the far end of campus, not far from where the house used to stand. It was torn down years ago. I'm not sure why, but probably after a prolonged slump in fraternity membership. The athletic fields remain in place. The track stadium still revels in its wooden, hundred year old design. The old basketball arena has been replaced by a new sleeker stadium on the other end of town. I'm not sure if the old building has any purpose any longer. And across the street, nothing can or will ever change the cemetery, which sits, as it has since before the Civil War; one securely fixed point in the changing ages.

Molly, who always walks a half-step ahead of me, turns to see what must be my facial expression of misunderstood awe, "Nostalgic?" she asks.

"I'm not sure," I answer.

"You're positive you want to do this?"

I look up to see our family, standing on the corner, waiting for us to complete the group. "In for a dime, in for a dollar," I tell my wife.

Mary, my oldest daughter, asks as we meet, "A lot's changed, huh, Dad?"

"Maybe," I say to her.

We turn on University Avenue and walk toward the center of

campus.

It is a crisp, fall Saturday, still dry. The monsoon season hasn't hit yet, but it will, and it will rain until April, as it does every year. As I look around, I wonder if the more time that goes by, the less things change. There is a banner strung between the street's light posts advertising Homecoming 2013. It is exactly the same as the one which read Homecoming 1970.

"What's the matter, Grandfather?" Tony, my astute, eight-year-old grandson asks.

"I just thought of someone," I tell him.

"Who?"

I quickly remember the person I once was and tell him, "Someone who lived here a long time ago."

Molly stops with me, takes my arm, and pats me gently on my wrist. She is the only person who could ever know what I am thinking.

"You guys go on to the luncheon," I tell the family. "I'll catch up with you later."

"I don't think the committee is going to like that, Dad," Ellen, my middle daughter says.

"Well, if nothing else, at least I'll be consistent."

My family walks down the slight hill towards the student union. I stand alone on the sidewalk and picture in my mind a young man in his prime, full of piss, promise, and great expectations, but mostly full of himself. Everyone knew him as Touchdown Tony McIntyre.

*JIM STEVENS*

**NOVEMBER 1970**

## CHAPTER 1

Homecoming Week.

Stupid concept. The only real reason they have homecoming is to sell out the football game, something they seldom did until I got here. Money, that's what it's all about. Suck in as much money as you can by staging events for old, rich, slap-on-the-back alumni to greet fellow old, rich, Pioneer alumni they can't remember, or don't want to remember. And while it's all going down, the university powers-that-be, mill around, putting the arm on people to donate anything from a new building to five bucks for some minority program nobody cares about—except the three or four minorities in the group. It is the one weekend of the year when the band has clean uniforms, the campus is spotless, and the townies stage a parade on the main drag, so every store can sell football souvenirs and paraphernalia—almost all of which has my picture or name emblazoned across it. I don't make a dime from any of it.

Just wait until it's my turn.

The kickoff event, no pun intended, is a noon rally on Monday, held at the student union. There must be a thousand people in front of the outdoor stage and hundreds more inside the building pressed against the eight-foot plate glass windows. I'm standing inside the union with the rest of the team, waiting to make our big entrance. We all wear ugly green sport coats, tan slacks, and bright gold ties; standard dress code to make us look like we have brains as well as brawn. Truth be told, most of the guys on the team have to have someone help tie their ties; these are the students who receive the scholarships.

The head cheerleader, Beth, or Betty or Brenda—I can't

remember names too well—has the tightest ass on campus. The only one even close in comparison is her twin sister's. I know this from personal experience. I had her *cheering for more* the night we beat Utah 36-3.

Beth and her cheer-buddies are on the stage, spinning and tossing each other around like pizza pie dough, as the worst band in the history of college marching bands toots their horns and bangs their drums in a rhythm all their own. Thank God there are only two games left in the regular season, because now every time I hear *Oh Pioneers*, I want to heave.

Pioneers lead us forward
Onto the battlefield.
Let us fight in all your glory
With your courage and ideals.
May the actions of our warriors
Emulate your spirit here.
Onto the field of victory,
March the fighting Pioneers.

"And here they are, the 1970 Fighting Pioneers," Betty wails into the microphone.

The crowd goes wild as the team takes the stage.

I always find it interesting, the second stringers, the special teams, the managers, and the water boys, in other words, the guys who never play, come out first, like they're the stars. They bounce out smiling, shuckin' and jivin', like the cat's meow. I don't care. Let them have their few moments in the spotlight. The best is always saved for last.

The defensive team prances out next. Most of them are black, colored, or whatever they call themselves this week. They aren't bad guys. They don't have that *we ain't taking no more bullshit* attitude like a lot of blacks who hang around campus like they own the place have. Mostly, the blacks on the team keep to themselves. They eat together, take a corner of the locker room, and listen to their own music on their 8-track players. I do find it interesting how the coaches treat them differently than they treat us. Like, they won't let the black guys wear afro hair-dos, which makes a lot of them pissed. Maybe they do that to make them meaner on the field. Who knows? Who cares? Personally, I think getting all that hair inside a helmet is more trouble than it's worth. As long as the defense can make the stops and keep us in the game, that's all I care about.

The offense comes out last and gets the loudest cheer from the crowd. Lester Tollinger, a one-man gang who has the IQ of a retarded Labrador, dances out, leading his buddies. He flails and flexes his arms and legs, like one of those zombies in *Night of the Living Dead.* The crowd loves Lester. I don't. I think he looks like the idiot he is, but I have to be nice to him since he is the offensive tackle who protects me in the pocket.

Lester brings the crowd close to a fevered pitch. Brenda takes over the microphone and announces, "And here he is, a junior from the State of Washington, the heart and soul of the Pioneers, Touchdown Tony McIntyre."

And, as usual, the crowd goes into a frenzy.

I take one step, but a hand clutches my arm, holding me back for just enough time to allow two massive posters to unfurl from the roof of the student union. It's forty-feet of me in all my glory, arm cocked, ball in hand, about to throw another perfect spiral for six points.

Now, it's bedlam.

Cheerleader Beth/Betty/Brenda gives me a huge smile, leads me to the microphone on the stand, and stays draped on my left shoulder. I call out to my fans, "Come on, let me hear you!"

The band pipes up another rendition of *Oh Pioneers*. Some in the crowd sing, some scream, some dance, and all applaud. The players behind me suck the adulation up like new kitchen sponges. I can see their heads swelling.

I raise my hands like Jesus, before he announced his free loaves and fishes lunch. "What are we going to do next

Saturday?" I cry out.

"Win."

"What?" I ask, cupping my hand behind my ear.

"Win." The answer comes back louder.

"I'm sorry," I say. "I didn't hear you."

"WIN!"

I raise my hands once more so they quiet, and can hear what I have to say. "I want to thank all of you for coming out today and coming out next Saturday to see us beat the crap out of Northern."

Applause, applause, applause. Cheers, cheers, cheers.

I'm about to continue, but I'm interrupted by a drum beat, one not coming from some idiot in the band. The beat gets louder. This isn't right. I look out, past the far edge of the throng of fans, and see a small group of students, way, way in the back. They're chanting to the beat of the drum, "All we are saying..."

"Hey, you back there," I call out, then pause.

"...is give peace a chance."

"This is a football rally," I inform them.

The chanting continues.

I see to my right, my Alpha Tau, frat brothers, already drunk from squirting boda-bag liquor into each other's mouths, turn to the offending group and start yelling and swearing at the offenders.

"Hey, shut up back there," I order to no avail.

"All we are saying...."

"You can do your protesting some other time," I try to reason with the group. "But this is about football."

"...is give peace a chance."

The drum continues along with the chant. I see the Alpha Taus head in the direction of the protestors. "You people can protest after the game on Saturday," I continue to try to reason with the idiots, "but right now all we care about is beating Northern."

"All we are saying...."

8

The rally on the stage abruptly stops. The whole team, cheerleaders, band, and a lot of the crowd, stand flat-footed, watching the protesters lock their arms together and continue to chant, "...is give peace a chance."

Lester Tollinger bumps me to the side sending Beth off my shoulder and onto the stage floor. "Shut... the... fuck... up," is Lester's subtle message into the microphone.

"All we are saying..."

Lester comes off the stage and rushes toward the protesters, followed by his fellow linemen. The crowd parts like the Red Sea to let them through. I'm about to join the posse, but a set of hands holds me back.

"Don't do it, Tony, you can't get hurt." It's my halfback Arthur, one of the few members of the team that actually takes classes to become something after he graduates, talking sense into my ear.

It doesn't take a lot of convincing for me to stay on stage. I stop. I know a mob has no brains and just heads. The mountain of football flesh reaches the arm-in-arm protesters.

It isn't pretty. Lester and the linemen, helped by drunken frat brats, go through the peace-lovers like a tornado through a trailer park. The locked arms are ripped apart, the circle separated, and bodies are tossed around like Frisbees at a frat picnic. The drum is destroyed. Love beads are ripped from necks. Tie-dyed shirts are torn to shreds. The already hyped up crowd, now acting as if they're ringside at a prize fight, screams for a knockout. The protesters hold to their belief of giving peace a chance, but their theory doesn't work. The protesters get hammered. Their bodies careen into one another like junk cars at a demolition derby. Protesters are slapped, stomped, and spat upon. Lester heaves one person after another in a mock hammer throw, each one achieving a new record in the human projectile category.

I can only hope the fight on the field next Saturday will be this easy to win.

It all ends when there is no one left to punish. Each protestor has run, limped, or crawled to the safety of a campus building or classroom.  Lester and buddies stand, victorious in a pack, like coyotes after a kill, and let loose with a frightening rebel yell, which puts an exclamation point to the end of the kick-off event.

What a great start for Homecoming Week.

## CHAPTER 2

Tuesday nights are reserved for in-house drinking. These inebriation events are much different than our more traditional drinking party, the *Friday at 4*, where we invite a sorority over, try to get them drunk, and into our rooms upstairs for some much-needed, end-of-week nookie. On Tuesday nights, the keg is only for the Alpha Taus. The brothers can get drunk, obnoxious, and stupid out of the view of gossipy sorority girls who love to make bad reputations even worse.

During the season I don't drink, or at least I don't drink much, but I still party. I love watching the freshmen and sophomores get blasted, and juniors and seniors make fools out of them. One of the more popular amusements is to set up six empty kegs in a triangle shape at one end of the party room. Two upperclassmen grab a drunken lower classman by his arms and legs, and sling him butt-first down the slick, beer-soaked floor in a human bowling competition. Steve Carlton, my bro buddy in the house, and I never lose a match. We have three perfect games to our credit. Nobody can beat us. If this sounds stupid and childish, it is. If it sounds painful, it is, but only if you are the slingee, and not the slinger.

College is fun. I wonder how much I'm going to miss it when I blow out of here.

---

Education for a college football player is different than education for people who go to college to get educated. The main reason for football players to go to college is to play football. With the exception of Arthur, and a few of the second string players I don't pay much attention to, a football player's only educational goal is to maintain a 2.0 grade point average. It's all we have to do to stay on the field. In order to achieve this high level of accomplishment, we enroll in what are referred to as Mickey classes, named after Disney's famous rodent.

Mickeys are the easiest classes offered each term. Each are worth three credits; and you seldom have to show up in class, don't have to do homework, or your homework is easily done by someone else. Sometimes there is a final, most times not.

And how do you find such classes? Well, besides the list on the locker room bulletin board, it's an unwritten law all athletes exchange information on which classes to take. The joke is that we all take basket weaving, but basket weaving is only offered as a summer term elective, and none of us ever go to summer school.

The problem is, not all the classes are Mickeys. The university forces you to take some required classes, like English and math; stuff you're never going to use. It seems dumb to me, but that's the rules.

The preferred plan is to take the minimum amount of units per term, be sure you get enough B's to offset the D's, and most importantly never get an F, because you get no credits for an F. You have to have fourteen, or maybe it's fifteen, credits passed each term. No big deal.

This being a state university, they set the bar pretty low. And, as a total stopgap measure, the athletic department assigns players who they really need on the field with tutors to assure at least a D in any class taken. It is said that you really have to work hard to flunk out of Pioneer U.

I'm in Shakespeare class. I sit in the middle, in the back, so I can watch this girl who has dark, brown hair down to her waist, a really nice ass, and wears high, lace-up boots even when it's not raining. Her name is Shelly or Sherry or Sharon. It's fun seeing how often I can get her to look my way.

"Double, double, toil and trouble. Fire burn and cauldron bubble." Professor Ringly stops reading, and must look my way because he says, "Getting a lot out of my lecture, Mr. McIntyre?"

The entire class turns towards me, except Shelly.

"Not yet," I tell my teacher, "but I'm planning on it."

12

At this instant, Sherry looks my way, I give her a smile, but she immediately averts her eyes. I like them shy, because once they are out of their little shell, they open up like a run defense against a play-action pass.

The bell rings. Another forty-five minutes of my life wasted.

"Papers are due Friday," RIngly says as the class packs up to leave.

On my way out of the classroom, I look up and see Sharon returning my smile.

---

Ruthie is the cook at the Alpha Tau house. She comes in around ten to get the kitchen going for the day. She whips up a soup, puts out luncheon meats, tuna salad, or whatever she could buy on sale Monday, which is when she shops for the week. Lunch starts at 11:30 am. Ruthie's a good cook, so good the hippie mailman Fred, and Max, the milkman, both schedule their deliveries at lunchtime.

You can eat anytime between 11:30 am and 1 pm, but if you want a lot, you get there before noon.

Everyone eats in the kitchen. If there isn't a stool available, you eat standing up. There always seems to be a lively discussion going on during mid-day meals. Today is no exception.

As I walk in, Fred spouts out clam chowder spittle, as he argues, "It's a war we can't win."

"Bullshit," Steve Carlton screams back.

"It's bullshit because there's nothing for us to win," Fred replies, as he tucks his long mane of hair into his shirt collar so it won't fall into his soup.

"America has never lost a war, and it won't lose this one." Steve seems especially demonstrative because he's wearing his ROTC uniform; a one-day a week fashion must for the future left-tenant.

Ralph and his roommate Ernie, both of whom had way too much to drink last night, offer their four cents to the discussion.

Ralph says, "They should draft Kung Fu. He'd kick some major Vietnam butt."

Ernie replies, "You don't send a gook to kill other gooks. You send John Wayne."

"Gooks always beat up other gooks," Ralph further explains, "like that Bruce Lee guy."

Steve jumps back in, "All I know is if Vietnam falls, Cambodia falls. If Cambodia falls, Thailand falls. And if Thailand falls, the commies control all of Southeast Asia."

"Who cares?" Fred asks.

"Somebody has to protect freedom and democracy in the world," Steve answers.

"Let somebody else do it."

Ruthie surprises all of us when she enters the conversation. "My son says the Vietnamese just want to be left alone."

Steve ignores her comment. He points his finger at Fred, as if he's pointing a gun. "What we should do is nuke 'em, and finish this thing in one fell swoop."

Fred asks, "You want to nuke 'em into peace?"

"Peace with honor."

"You're demented."

I never get into these discussions. What's the point? I start in on the chowder.

Steve asks Fred, "Whose side are you on, anyway?"

"The right side."

"There is no right side," Steve says, "only our side."

"We don't know what the hell we're doing over there," Fred says.

"That's why we elect leaders in this country, who know more about this than you do, and who will make the right decisions."

"Tricky Dick Nixon is a bigger liar than Lyndon Johnson," Fred says. "If that's even possible."

"Presidents don't lie to the people who elected them."

Fred finishes his chowder, takes what's left of his sandwich, hefts his mailbag onto his shoulder, and says before leaving the

14

kitchen, "Everybody is lying, that's what the Sixties are all about."

Wow, that was deep, I think as I load up a sandwich.

Ruthie asks Steve, "You don't think they lied to my Jerry, do you?"

Steve ignores her again, but I ask her, "Did you get a letter this week?"

"Not yet."

"Don't worry, you will."

Steve sits, still in a stew, hotter than his clam chowder. "Ruthie, tell Fred to mooch his lunch someplace else. He ain't our kind."

## CHAPTER 3

Practice. I hate practice.

The defense takes the south end of the field. The offense takes the north. The band lines up just to the edge of the end zone. Last week, one of my passes got tipped, went screwy, hit a trombone player, and the guy lost two front teeth.

Our head coach, Darryl Praytel, believes he's an offensive genius. He's offensive, but hardly a genius. Praytel has the play calling creativity of a second-string, third grade QB in a Pop Warner league. He has developed our offense into a three-step, drop back, quick slant, five-to-ten yard passing extravaganza. When we run the ball, it's always a quick, off-tackle burst for five yards. I think the offensive plan is pure bullshit. I seldom get to throw the ball more than ten yards. But it works. Our record is the best it's been in years, and Praytel is riding my throwing arm to what he thinks is going to be a big fat NFL contract.

Arthur comes into the huddle, "Run X 16, off-tackle, left."

I look over to Praytel, then back at the players around me. "Run X 4 Z out, left."

"That's not what Coach Praytel called," Arthur corrects me.

Lester adjusts his jock. "Fuck, God-damned Praytel."

"Do you have to swear every time you open your mouth?" Arthur asks Lester.

"Fuck no," Lester replies.

"On two."

The huddle breaks. We line up against the redshirt/second string defense.

Praytel notices the wrong formation immediately. "What the hell do you think you're doing?" he screams from the sideline.

"Hut, hut."

The ball is snapped. I drop back, fake right to the tight end, hesitate, and throw a perfect sixty-yard spiral to the split end down the left sideline. Touchdown.

Praytel storms onto the field, blowing his whistle, louder than a lifeguard trying to get kids out of a pool. "What the hell is going on?"

I stay calm, telling him, "I audibled."

"You don't audible in practice."

"Why not?"

"Same reason you don't audible in a game," Praytel gets right into my facemask. "Because I say you don't."

"I want to call my own plays."

"Forget it."

"I'm the quarterback."

"So what?"

"I'm on the field. I can see more than you. I should call my own plays." The team circles as Praytel and I go at it.

Praytel grabs my face guard, pulls me like a dog on a leash away from the team. "Listen, if you think I'm going to trust my career to your feeble brain, you're wrong, boy."

"I should call my own plays." I don't give up easily.

Praytel holds his hands against the side of my helmet, forcing me into his bad breath. "Don't think. You are not out here to think. You listen, you repeat, you execute. You understand?"

"I think..."

He slaps both hands hard against the side of my helmet.

Ouch.

"You didn't get this far on the basis of your I.Q." Praytel informs me before he pushes me back to the team. "Now, run X 16 off tackle, or you'll all be doing full pad, wind sprints until game time next Saturday."

Is it any wonder I hate practice?

---

I carry a tennis ball everywhere I go. I squeeze it in my right hand, hundreds of times every day. Sometimes I toss it, catch it, toss it, catch it. It's all about strong hand, sharp eye, coordination.

Marcus Jones is waiting for me in the library.

"You're late."

"Sorry Mark."

"It's Marcus."

I sit across from him at a table in the middle of the study room, a place I don't feel very comfortable. "How'd you ever get the name Marcus?"

"Marcus Garvey."

"Was he the father you never knew?"

"He was a famous civil rights leader."

"Colored guy or black guy?"

"Actually, he was a Negro."

"You guys should all get together and decide what you want to be called."

My tutor takes a deep breath and asks, "Where's your books?"

"I forget."

"Makes it a bit difficult for me to do my job."

"Then can I go?"

"No."

"I got a friend picking me up in a few minutes." I lean back in the chair and toss the tennis ball in the air.

"You know," he tells me, "I don't want to be here anymore than you do."

"So, can we both go?"

"No." Marcus opens a small calendar book. "You do the English paper due on Friday?"

"I'm working on getting it done."

"How?"

"With a great amount of personal effort."

Marcus leans back, gives me his favorite look of frustration, as I toss the tennis ball.

I ask, "So, what are we going to do, sit here and look stupid for an hour?"

"That certainly would be no problem for you."

18

"Good one, Marcus. You really devastate me with your sarcastic wit."

Marcus tries to catch the tennis ball on its way down, but I snatch it before he can. I'm way too quick for him. "Don't you care about anything, Tony?"

"Football. I care about football."

"Anything besides football?" He asks, then says, "You are in college, if you don't remember."

I stop tossing and lean toward him. "Me reading about some Shakespeare, Big Mac bitches, or why X minus 2 equals bupkis, isn't going to help me read an NFL defense."

"The purpose of a college education is to teach you how to think."

"That's exactly what everybody's telling me not to do."

A not-very-attractive girl, a table or two away with a stack of books in front of her, shushes us. Marcus apologizes with a wave of his hand.

"Why can't we do this in my room?" I ask.

"I like libraries."

"Why? You can't talk, you can't eat, and there's no TV."

"Precisely."

"Wow. Big word."

"Listen," Marcus is getting pissed. "If you think I'm going to lose my scholarship because you don't want to be here, you're mistaken. This is part of my deal, I don't have a choice."

"And that's *my* problem?" I ask.

I restart my tennis ball tossing. I catch about three before one of us speaks.

"I saw you on campus the other day, Marcus. You get paid to pass out that peace and love bullshit?"

"No."

"Then why do you do it?"

"Because it's the right thing to do."

"Who was that girl with you?"

"None of your business."

19

"She was one piece of prime poontang." I say, raising my eyebrows.

"Shut up."

"She's whiter than a bleached hospital sheet."

"Shut up, Tony."

"You like salt? She like pepper?" I ask.

"I said, shut up."

"When you two go out on a date, she sits in the front of the bus, while you sit in the back?"

Marcus slams his calendar book shut. "Screw you, Tony."

He's pissed. I hit a nerve, a big nerve, and now I got him.

"You gonna get up and punch me out, Marcus? Show me whose boss?"

Marcus' big nostrils are pumping in the air. "You think I like doing this, Tony?" He snaps back at me. "Sitting here, trying to help some jerk, who could care less about what's important in life?"

"And you're going to tell me what's important in my life?"

"Maybe if you tried listening for a change," Marcus says.

"Guess what, Marcus?" I lean toward him one last time. "I don't give a shit about you, about some English paper, about listening to anybody." I pause before I ask, "You know what's important to me, Marcus?"

He doesn't answer.

"Winning. That's all anybody cares about. Me, students, alumni, idiots in the stands, all anyone cares about is if we beat Northern on Saturday. That's it. No more, no less." I look him straight in the eye. "I got the weight of the whole university on my shoulders. I don't have time to give a shit about anything else."

Marcus gives me a long stare. He's at the end of his rope. He's done. "Just get out of here. I don't want to have to look at you any longer."

I stand. I smile. I say, "You might not think I'm very bright, Marcus, but I sure know how to play you." And I leave.

Sure got a lot out of that session.

20

---

Steve Carlton drives a Dodge Dart with a three-on-the-tree transmission. He's parked in the alley behind the library.

"I got to pick up Cindy," he informs me as I sit shotgun.

"Do we have to?"

"Yes, you do that when you're in love."

"I wouldn't know."

He grinds the gears as we take off.

Steve's girlfriend, Cindy, is a local girl who lives on the other side of town. Cindy's mom died of cancer of something a few years ago, so Cindy lives at home taking care of her dad, or vice-versa. I'm not real wild about Cindy.

Cindy and Steve have been going out since they were both freshmen. Cindy's not bad looking. She's about 5'6", got a nice ass, cute tits, and bottle blond hair. If you look up *Small Town Beauty Queen* in the dictionary, you'll see Cindy's picture. She's one of those girls without a wrinkle. Her clothes are always flawlessly ironed. She wears a lot of dresses and outfits that match. None are very sexy. I don't think she owns a pair of jeans. And, if she's wearing boots, she always has a regular pair of shoes to change into when she goes inside. Cindy has a ton of friends. Whenever I see her on campus, there's always a bunch of chicks around her. Seldom are any of the girls hanging around her better looking than Cindy. She runs Steve ragged. She's always got some event to drag him to, where she ends up working the room, and Steve wanders off not knowing what to do. Cindy's the rules chairwoman of her sorority, plays the flute, and brags about attending lectures the Philosophy Department puts on.

Cindy's not my type, which is about every type, except Cindy's type. She's a control freak, which I can't handle. She never lets up. Tells Steve what to wear, what to say, who to talk to. What a pain in the ass, but as long as it is Steve's ass, and not mine, I really don't care. I don't know why he puts up with it.

The most interesting aspect of Steve and Cindy's relationship, which Steve thinks I'm the only one in the house who knows about it, is their sex life, or actually the absence of a sex life. Cindy won't let Steve screw her. Maybe it's a religious thing, or she's saving herself for marriage, or she's frigid; who knows? Who cares? I think it's pretty funny. Steve's tried everything. Getting her drunk, threatening to dump her, telling her he's going to go out and buy it, but nothing works. He's as horny as a kennel-kept cocker spaniel penned next to a bitch in heat. If I were Steve, my nuts would have busted by now.

Steve works for Cindy's old man, Diamond Jim Bradley. This guy is a real piece of work. He's in his fifties, but looks mid-sixties, chain smokes, has a huge beer gut, dyes what hair he's got left black, and does this comb-over that makes it look like he's got stripes going over his lily-white skull. Everybody in town knows Diamond Jim, because he's the star of his agency's TV commercials. On TV, he makes obnoxious, used car salesmen look dull. "If it's insurance you need, see Diamond Jim Bradley."

I have only been in the house a few times, but if Diamond Jim is home, he's in his favorite chair, in front of the TV, martini in hand, watching the news or a sporting event. Diamond Jim loves sports. He can talk your ear off about any game from baseball to tetherball, roller derby to wrestling. If people are in the room with him, having a chat on another topic, it's not odd to hear Diamond Jim belt out comments like, "That could go for extra bases," or "You got him hurt, so finish him off." Diamond Jim never takes his eyes off the TV. An earthquake could hit and Diamond Jim would be too busy watching a goal line stand to care.

Diamond Jim loves it when Steve brings me by, which is exactly what is going on right now. He'll start in on me about the strategy for the game Saturday, how much we'll win by, or if Praytel is going to let me open it up and throw the ball downfield. I give him bullshit answers which he's not smart enough to realize they're bullshit. Tomorrow, when he's trying to sell a sucker some crummy annuity policy, he'll drop into the conversation, "I was talking with Tony McIntyre last night..." Everybody makes money off Touchdown Tony, except Tony.

As we go up the walk, Duke, the Bradley's German shepherd is barking up a storm, trying to break out the front door and get at us. Always nice to feel welcomed. I hear Diamond Jim scream at the dog, "Duke, shut up." And Duke quiets. Cindy comes to the door with a fresh martini in hand and lets us in. She lets Steve kiss her on her cheek.

We walk into the front room. The News is on the TV. Cindy hands her dad his second, third, maybe fourth martini of the night.

"Tony, my man. Good to see you."

"Hey there, Diamond Jim."

"What are you watching?" Cindy asks her dad.

We all pause to see a helicopter in Vietnam evacuate wounded soldiers as bullets fly and shells explode. "There were nine Americans killed and sixty-four Viet Cong casualties," the voiceover of the story says. There is a close-up of an American, whose leg has been severed at the knee and is bleeding profusely, a shot of two guys bleeding from their chests, and one guy dead on the stretcher. Gruesome, to say the least.

"Kill them Commies," Diamond Jim blurts out.

"Can't we watch something else?" Cindy asks daddy.

Diamond Jim exchanges his empty martini glass for a full one, and clicks the remote.

A boxing match pops onto the TV screen.

"How about a couple of niggers beating the crap out of each other?" Diamond Jim asks.

"They're not niggers anymore, Daddy, they're black people."

"Blacks, niggers, coons, jig-a-boos, they're all the same to me," Daddy answers daughter.

"But if one wanted to buy insurance, you'd sell it to him?" I toss into the conversation.

"No," Jim says. "Steve would sell it to him because I'm making him head of our nigger division."

"Then I want a raise," Steve says.

Diamond Jim pumps a raised thumb into the air. "I'll give you a raise."

"Daddy, do you always have to be so rude to Steve?"

"Yes."

I check the grandfather clock in the hallway. "We've got to get going or we're going to miss dinner," I say to Steve.

"Cindy, we got to go," Steve says to Cindy.

"You got to drop me at the Legion," Diamond Jim informs us.

"We don't have time, Daddy."

"You always have time for your daddy, Princess." Diamond Jim finishes the martini in one gulp, stands up, adjusts his belt under the middle of his belly pouch, and kicks the dog towards the back door. "Out, Duke, out."

Outside, I don't say a word when Diamond Jim sits shotgun, and Cindy and I have to sit in the back. Once we're on the road, I look over at Cindy's bare knee and wonder what would happen if I put my hand over it, and slid it slowly down her thigh, but even I'm not that much of a jerk.

"You close that Dalloway policy today?" Diamond Jim asks Steve.

Steve replies, "He said he wanted to think it over."

"Jesus Christ, you're not there to let him think," Diamond Jim yells across the front seat.

"I'll get him to sign, don't worry about it."

"You better."

"Watch out!" I blurt out from the back seat, as I see a dog run across the road in front of us. Cindy screams. Steve slams on the brakes. Tires squeal. Diamond Jim crashes forward into the front console. The car swerves to the right and misses the dog, which continues to run across the street, only to get slammed by a Ford Falcon coming in the opposite direction.

"Where the hell you learn how to drive?" Diamond Jim yells at Steve.

The dog howls in pain lying on the other side of the road.

"Stop, stop," Cindy yells through her tears.

24

"Don't stop!" Diamond Jim orders.

"Stop, Steve, the dog is hurt."

"No, keep going."

Steve must choose between money and love. He picks money. The Dart continues down the road.

"We just can't leave the dog there. It's going to die," Cindy says, looking back at the wounded animal.

"What the hell are you going to do?" Daddy questions daughter. "Go over there and give it artificial reparation?"

Steve grinds the gearshift into second gear.

"That was horrible, I'm going to have nightmares," Cindy says as her mascara runs down her face in rivulets.

"Watch where the hell you're going," Diamond Jim says to Steve.

"It wasn't my fault."

"Damn dog deserved to get hit," Diamond Jim sums up the incident.

We all take a moment to catch our breath.

"Ya know," I say, "I don't get it. You see soldiers getting slaughtered on TV and it doesn't bother you a bit, but when a dumb dog gets hit in the street, you freak out."

Cindy quits crying, turns to me and says, "One's on TV, Tony, and one is real."

Wow, she told me.

We drop off Diamond Jim at the American Legion Hall and Cindy at the Delta-Delta house. We get to our house and the bros are already at the dinner table. Steve takes his seat, next to the president, Rick Snyder. Steve is the House Manager, the guy who budgets, pays the bills, orders the supplies, gets stuff fixed, and tells Ruthie what to cook. I always sit at the end of the table, closest to the kitchen door, so when the extras are bought out, I get first crack.

Dinner is Salisbury steak, which isn't steak, but cheap, mystery meat covered with thick sauce. The sides are green beans and mashed potatoes. I'm surprised we all don't grow extra eyes with the amount of mashed potatoes we get around here. Thank God, I get to eat training table three nights a week. Ruthie made lemon cake for dessert.

At the conclusion of every dinner, a tacky gong is sounded and President Rick says, "Announcements."

"We need more toilet paper," Ralph starts off.

"No," Steve tells him.

"We don't have enough," Ralph adds, and is immediately backed up by the voices of most of the members.

"This house uses more toilet paper than a diarrhea ward," Steve responds to the growing rabble.

"We still need more," is heard repeatedly.

"I got a budget," Steve explains.

"I got skid marks on all my jockeys."

"I got a rash. Anyone want to see?"

The conversation quickly becomes a screaming match between Steve and the brothers. It ends when Rick bangs the gong and tells the brothers, "All right, shut up."

Sean, a sophomore, waits until the room quiets, and speaks in a soft, conversational tone, "I was passing by the SAE House the other day, and they told me that the Alpha Taus were nothing but a bunch of dirty assholes. And I couldn't argue with them."

The shouting starts again. I look up to see Ruthie signaling me from the kitchen door. I get up and follow her into the kitchen.

One look at the visitor and I ask, "What are you doing here?"

My mother, Verna, stands with a notebook in her hand.

"I have something for you."

"You know I hate it when you come here."

She hands me the notebook. "Learn these for Saturday."

"You promised me you wouldn't stop in like this."

"Quiet."

I won't take the notebook from her hand, but she keeps pushing it towards me. I don't have much choice.

"Read them."

I'm going to read them anyway, so I might as well read them

26

now. As I page through the notebook, Ruthie says to my mother, "I'm Ruthie, the cook."

Mom tells her, "Tony needs more protein in his diet."

I cut off their conversation. "I'm not going to show Praytel these plays."

"Why not?"

"Because he's not going to let me run any of them."

"Why not?"

"Because he's an asshole."

"Learn them anyway."

"Why?"

"Don't argue with me, Tony. Learn the plays."

I hate it when she shows up like this. It's a three hour drive to get here, and she has to leave Dad by himself while she's gone. It was bad enough in high school when she wouldn't leave the coach alone, but now I'm in college; it's embarrassing.

Ruthie asks my mother, "What kind of protein?"

"You're the cook, lady, you pick. I can't do everything."

## CHAPTER 4

I like women a lot. And I like a lot of women, a lot more.

A lot of it probably has to do with that Darwin thing, where the fittest species are supposed to mate with the other fittest species, but I'm not so sure, because it doesn't make sense why so many chicks take the pill, or ask me to use a rubber.

I thought I got a lot of girls in high school, but it's nothing compared to what I get in college. And they're not only cheerleaders or the horny little bad girls. A lot of the chicks I bang in college are the goody-goody, puritanical types, who aren't supposed to be *giving it away* or *jumping in the sack* for a one-night stand.

Having sex with a lot of women, teaches you a lot about women. One rule I follow is never spend too much time trying to convince a girl to have sex. Make it clear right away what's going to happen, and if she doesn't immediately respond with a cute little smile or wink, move on. Women are like footballs at practice, there's always another one to throw around. If I'm really horny, and I want to get laid right away, I have a fool-proof method. In a bar or at a party, I don't go after the most attractive girl in the group, but hit on the number two or number three in the pack. These girls are so thrilled to be picked before numero uno, they'll do just about anything. I have no real preferences when it comes to hair color, although I do sense blondes are dumber than brunettes. Redheads are especially fun when their purses match their shoes. Girls with jet-black hair should always wear it straight to the middle of their back.

Another rule I follow is: Never talk about sex with someone when you are having sex with somebody else. Nobody likes to be compared, especially during or after the act; although I compare all my partners. Why not? We are ranked and compared our entire lives. From report cards in school, to shooting percentages in basketball, to quarterback ratings in football, there is a set standard for every activity. Why should sex be any different? I'm not a *one-to-ten* rater type, but more of an *all are good, some are better,* kind of a guy. Although, I will say it has been my experience that girls, which are 10's on the looks scale, seldom rank as high on the sex scale. This is always disappointing, but I've learned to live with it. The most fun sexually is to be surprised. Like she's real shy and reserved meeting her, but once the clothes come off, she turns into a sex machine. Just like in football, the element of surprise should never be discounted.

When you are the star of the football team, you get your share of women. You also get a lot of other guy's shares. This isn't fair, but when it comes to sex, nobody ever said it was going to be fair. It's different for guys than it is for girls. Guys are supposed to have a lot of women. Women, on the other hand, are supposed to be particular on who they sleep with, but this doesn't make sense either. Somebody told me once college guys have sex with an average of eight girls in their four years, and college co-eds average three, which comes out in the wash that a few college girls must be doing one hell of a lot of college guys. I think when it comes to sex, guys lie about how many they get, and girls lie about how few they've had.

Guys have no problem asking me how much sex I have. Girls usually hint around, trying to find out. I never tell. I always try to turn it around when the question comes up.

"Have you had a lot of women, Tony?" some chick might ask.

"How many do you consider a lot?" I ask instead of answer.

"A hundred?"

"Per year or total?" I question, which always ends the questioning.

---

"Did you read it?" she asks.

"No."

"Read the Cliff Notes?"

"No."

Shelly/Sherry/Sharon has her black boots on, which are really sexy. Her hair is down to her waist; it's shiny and as smooth as silk. She wears a black, turtle-neck sweater, and a pair of tight jeans. I used to think her ass was her best feature, but I can now see her breasts give her ass a good run for the money.

I'm watching her from the bed where I'm squeezing a tennis ball in my right hand. "I was hoping you'd give me a quick summary and we could go from there."

"OK," she says, flips off the electric typewriter, and turns from the built in desk to face me. The room is small, I could easily reach out and touch her. "Macbeth is this General, who hears from three witches he's going to become King. And it goes to Macbeth's head, causing him to speed up the process by killing the existing King, a guy named Duncan."

"Wow, cold dude, that Macbeth."

"His wife loves her hubby being king, but Macbeth gets really paranoid, killing everyone who he thinks is after his throne. It gets pretty bloody. Lady Macbeth, his loony wife, gets even loonier, and commits suicide after walking around the castle at night with a candle. Then, Macbeth really goes off the deep end, and gets his head chopped off, which is carried onto stage in the last act."

"So, it's not a comedy?"

"Ah, no."

I take a moment to try to take it all in. It's quite a lot to swallow. I'm glad I didn't waste my time reading it. Sherry is looking better and better, but I better hold myself back.

"What's the paper supposed to be about?" I ask about the assignment *we're* working on.

"Theme," she says. "We're supposed to write about the main theme in Macbeth."

Sharon waits for me to say something, but I don't, because I have no clue.

"Obsessive ambition," she says.

"And that's a bad thing?"

"It is in Macbeth's case."

30

"What's so wrong about being ambitious?" I ask.

"Nothing, as long as you don't lose your head over it, like Macbeth did."

I think this over for a few seconds. "Could you write something up about how Macbeth's problem is not his ambition, but that he doesn't know how to channel his ambition in the right direction?"

"What do you mean?" she asks.

"Like, instead of just being satisfied being the king, Macbeth should have gone on to the next level, and put his ambition into bigger and better things."

"Like what?"

"Conquering other countries, or the world, like Attila the Hun did."

"Macbeth started a civil war, but that's where he got his head chopped off."

"So, if he would have picked on an easy country to conquer first, instead of biting off more than he could chew, he would have channeled his ambition much better."

"That's certainly a different take on the play."

"It's kinda like a football season. You want to start off playing lousier teams, get your confidence up beating the crap out of them before you take on teams in your division."

"Okay."

"And if Macbeth worked his way up, went undefeated, and took over the world, his wife probably wouldn't have done herself in, and the play could have had a happy ending."

"I don't think a happy ending was what Shakespeare was after here," she says.

"I'm thinking out of the box here. That's what you have to do to win sometimes. Do something that the other side would never think of."

"I see your point," she says, but I know she's not convinced. I don't really care.

"Could you maybe type something up along those lines?"

"I guess I could."

"Then could you put my name on the bottom and hand it in for me, because with the game on Saturday, I doubt if I'll be in class on Friday?" I quit squeezing the tennis ball, sit up, reach over, place my hand on the spot between her shoulder and her neck, and start to gently rub. "Please."

Before she's able to answer, I lean over and give her a kiss.

Here's another thing I've learned about women. Never kiss a woman hard the first time you kiss her. Be gentle. Don't force your tongue down her throat like a plumber unclogging a drain. Be nice. Ease into it. You want her to think you're really sensitive, because once she thinks that, you're in for the score. Once you get the first kisses out of the way, you can go hog wild on the bitch.

"I'd really appreciate you helping me out," I tell her in my softest tones and keep up the kissing, so she can't tell me "No."

It works.

Five minutes later, we're lying on the bed. In ten minutes, we're both naked. Fifteen minutes more and I pop the question. "Where are you in your cycle?"

"What?" Shelly asks, a bit taken out of her unbridled passion.

"Where are you in your cycle?" I ask again, but add some explanation to the question. "Neither of us wants an accident to happen."

Sherry doesn't answer. So I crawl off, get up, go to my desk drawer, scavenge around in the dark until I find one foil packet, bite the corner of it, rip it open, and climb back in next to her. Before putting it on, I start the sensitive kissing again to get Sharon back in the mood.

It works.

Ten minutes later, I'm done.

Before I can tell her how great she was—something I do with all the women I sleep with, even if they are lousy in the sack—the door opens, and Steve Carlton bursts into the room.

I must have forgotten to hang something on the outside door

32

knob.

"I can't fucking believe it," Steve shouts out, before seeing the two of us in bed.

"What's the matter this time?" I ask, propping myself up on one elbow.

Steve comes all the way into the room and sits on the chair where Shelly/Sherry/Sharon sat. "She still won't let me do her."

Shelly tucks the sheet and covers around her neck as she rests her head on the pillow.

"What'd you try this time?" I ask.

I've kept a running tab on all the ways Steve has tried to convince Cindy to screw him. Dinners, presents, getting her drunk, going to her family get-togethers, working for her old man, taking care of her dog, going to her sorority formal, and telling her he loves her. Nothing's worked. Me, I never do much more than buy a pizza.

"I gave her my pin," Steve tells us, as if he is admitting to a horrendous crime.

"What does that mean?" Sherry asks, seemingly intrigued by the idiocy of the situation.

"You're not in a sorority?" Steve asks her.

"No."

"It means I'm promising to ask her to marry me."

"And she still won't screw him," I explain to Sharon.

"Why not?"

"This time she said she couldn't because Miss Scarlet was paying her monthly visit."

I try not to laugh, but can't hold back. I have to muffle my face into the pillow, I'm laughing so hard.

"It happens," Shelly explains.

Steve, who sits, elbows on knees and head in his hands, rises his head up slowly, and says, "But it always happens to me."

"Timing is everything," I tell my horny, frat brother.

"It's not easy being a woman," Sharon says.

I quit laughing long enough to tell Steve, "Listen to Sherry, she knows what she's talking about."

My dark haired beauty gives me a not-so-pleasant look, "It's Shelly, not Sherry."

"Well, I got the S part right, didn't I?" I say with a smirk.

She doesn't laugh, must not have gotten my joke.

## CHAPTER 5

It's Friday, the day before we play Northern.

Banners are up, reading, "Welcome back Alumni." Signs hang in all the bars advertising drink specials during the parade. In store windows on Main Street there are t-shirts, sweatshirts, hats, rain ponchos, boots, gloves; you name it, they got it for sale, all with a Pioneer mascot or my picture prominently displayed. No matter where I go in the next few months, I'll see people wearing me.

The team has to report to the locker room this afternoon at five o'clock. They lock us up in a hotel the night before the game, to assure nobody goes out and gets drunk. They're too cheap to give us our own rooms, or they're scared we're going to smuggle some girl in, have sex, and zap our energy for the game; so, we have to double up. Arthur is my roommate. Praytel probably put us together thinking Arthur's *holier than thou* qualities will rub off on me. It hasn't worked so far. Lester is the only guy on the team that doesn't have to share a room, because every roommate he's ever had complained he farted so much during the night, they couldn't get any sleep. We'll get a big steak dinner and see a movie tonight. The movie is always about some guy or team who comes from behind to win the big game. Tomorrow morning we'll get to sleep in, have a big breakfast, and take a bus to the stadium, arriving about two hours before kickoff.

I'm at the student union, a little before 3 pm. It's media time. There is a stage set up with a table and two chairs. In front of each chair is six or seven microphones from the radio and TV stations, both in town and up in Portland. I sit in one of the chairs, and Praytel sits in the other. A guy named Larry, Lenny, or Lewis stands to the right, running the show by pointing to reporters in the audience to ask questions. Idiots ask the same questions, week after week after week.

"What's your prediction on the game, Tony?"

"I make touchdowns, not predictions."

"Do you think you have a shot at winning the Heisman this year?"

"I hope so."

"How good of a chance?"

"If I don't win it this year, I'll win next year."

"Is there any truth to the rumor that you may skip your senior year and opt for the NFL?"

"My education is very important to me. I plan to graduate from this university." I pause, then add, "And I just told you if I don't win the Heisman this year, there's always next year."

"The Pioneers are eight and two..."

Praytel cuts off the reporter to add, "The best record the school has had in sixteen seasons." Praytel gets pissed when all the questions come my way.

"As I was saying," the reporter continues, "if you win, and the California schools lose, you got a shot at the Rose Bowl. How important is that?"

"Not at all," Praytel answers. "All we care about is tomorrow. We don't worry about what we can't control."

Bullshit. Praytel would give his left nut to play in a bowl game, especially the Rose Bowl. A nationally televised, New Year's Day event with millions of people watching, who is he trying to kid? Hell, even if he loses, his stock in the coaching trade will skyrocket. He'd get big offers from bigger schools, or he could renegotiate his Pioneer contract for a much bigger chunk of change. To be honest, I feel the same way. Playing in the Rose Bowl could make Touchdown Tony a household name. It would up my status in the Heisman race, as well as pump up my number and price in next year's NFL draft.

"Tony, you've been playing the same tightly controlled, short pass offense all year, any thoughts on opening up the field to bigger plays?"

I feel a kick under the table before I answer. "All I want to do, is do what I have to do to win."

Praytel can't let this one go by without comment. "We'll be

playing Pioneer football, if anyone thinks we'd give up on what got us this far, they're nuts."

"Tony, any comment on the choice of Grand Marshall of the homecoming parade?"

"A better choice couldn't have been made."

There are a few more dumb questions asked, followed by dumb answers from Praytel. Louis or Lenny closes down the press conference, and all the reporters and cameramen pack up quickly.

I'm done for the day. I've got about two hours before I have to report in. I come off the stage and the most obnoxious reporter on the planet, Ace Dunnigan, sticks his microphone in my face and asks, "Rumor has it, you and Praytel aren't seeing eye-to-eye on the game plan tomorrow. Care to comment?"

I push his microphone away.

"I heard things got a little testy in practice this week." Ace won't back off. The jerk-off and his cameraman chase me down the hall. "Care to comment, Tony?"

I look up and see Marcus and his cute, little babe. I'll use Marcus to get this asshole off my back. "Marcus," I call out. "How are you doing?"

Marcus, who is loaded down with peace and love posters stops, hears his name, and turns toward me. "Tony?"

I pick up the pace. "Hey, Marcus, wait up." I rush the pair, leaving the ace reporter, Ace, in the dust with his hand still pointing the microphone my way.

Marcus walks into the office of one of those campus organizations I could care less about. "What do you want?" he asks.

"Hi, I'm Tony McIntyre," I introduce myself to Marcus' hot, white chick.

"Katie." She shakes my hand.

I smile. She smiles back.

"You write the Shakespeare paper and turn it in?" Marcus asks.

I look around to see all kinds of 'not my kind of people' doing all kinds of stuff I wouldn't do. The room filled with anti-war posters, paintings, bumper stickers, fliers, and a six-foot statue of a policeman flashing the peace sign. I don't know much about art, but I know this statue ain't art. "What the hell is that?"

"The artist calls it *Force of Peace*," Katie tells me.

"Looks like a forced piece a shit to me."

Katie smiles, Marcus frowns. "Did you do the paper or not, Tony?"

"The paper was done and I'm pretty sure it was handed in this morning."

I see out into the hallway, the coast is clear of obnoxious TV reporters. "Well, it's been a slice visiting with you, but I got to go. It was great to meet you Katie."

"It was nice meeting you."

"Why don't you have Marcus bring you along to one of our study sessions?"

"Okay."

I smile. She smiles back.

"Goodbye, Tony," Marcus says.

I walk back to the Alpha Tau house. The brothers are all outside drinking beer and decorating a truck for the parade tomorrow. I don't bother to go outside and say "hello." On my door are two messages my mother called, and one envelope she dropped off. Inside the envelope is yet another play, a sweep right, flare to the flat, and reverse pass. A play you'd run if you were playing touch football, but hardly major college material. I wonder where she comes up with this stuff.

I think about calling Shelly to drop by for a quickie, but that probably isn't a good idea. The Northern team is no pushover. I take out my playbook and re-read the game plan for tomorrow's offense, and the list of plays that will be the basis of our attack.

I report to the locker room at 5 pm.

---

Bus to the hotel, check in, unpack, and hang around; steak for dinner. After cherry pie, we sit around and wait for Lester to start blowing farts. Praytel gets up and introduces Doctor Ernst, Ernie, or Ernesto to speak to us about the *Power of Visual Thinking*. We all have to listen to this bonehead tell us how to picture in our minds the exact actions we will take on the field. Dr. Ernst says, "Before each play, visualize in your mind exactly what you want to do. See yourself in the actual play, as if it's a movie playing in your mind. See it. Feel it. Then do it."

This is stupid. What are we supposed to do, zone out into LaLa Land before every play? Don't you think it might make more sense if we see the defense they're running, or if they're going to blitz, or overload a zone? This Ernie guy is an idiot. And he's a wimp. I bet he's never played a down of football in his life.

Ernesto goes on and on about how you have to be visually acute in our thought processes during the game. "It is just as important to be mentally involved as physically involved."

Here's where Ernst' bullshit falls apart. A couple of guys on the team are almost retarded. So explain to me, Doctor, how mentally involved can they get, when they barely have enough brains to put on a uniform? Right now, the only guy in the room, in my opinion, dumber than Dr. Ernesto Visual, is Praytel.

Next, we get herded into a room where they put up one of those tacky movie screens, and we watch *Jim Thorpe, All American*. The movie is so old I'm surprised it even has sound. It's the story of this Indian football player, who played before they had helmets with faceguards. No wonder the guy was a little loony, he probably got banged in the head one too many times.

Old Jim Thorpe is like a total screw-up. He goes to the Olympics and wins all these medals, but he has to give them back, because he wasn't smart enough to hide the money he made playing baseball for some rinky-dink team. Then he plays professional football, but screws that up too, by drinking too much firewater. Next, he wants to coach a team, but no one wants him because he's such a loser. At the end of the movie, he's

39

a bum, driving a truck, wanting to coach a Pop Warner team. Talk about a dumb, unrealistic ending, my mother would have gone totally berserk if my Pop Warner coach were some bourbon belting, Indian derelict wearing a leather helmet. Whoever thought this movie was going to fire us up for the game tomorrow, must have been smoking way too much hippie love weed.

---

On the bus to the stadium, I'm two rows from the back, next to a window. The bus goes across town, left up Alder Street, past the Alpha Tau house, and right on University Avenue. We go past the cemetery, the old basketball stadium, athletic offices, and student union. At the intersection of Main and University, we stop to watch what's left of the parade.

On the reviewing platform, University President Bernard Schwartz and his wife wave as the Big Sound of the Valley, the Pioneer Band, marches past playing yet another encore of *Oh, Pioneers*. If I were the president, I would put a limit on how many times the song could be played in any 24 hour period. Next, is the Swallow Lumber float, which is a log truck refitted with a platform upon which the cheerleaders can cartwheel to their heart's content. Following the bouncing babes and boys is a garish, green and gold, convertible Bonneville Deuce-and-a-Quarter, driven by Cindy Bradley. Her daddy, Diamond Jim, is seated above the car's back seat, waving to his current and future customers. Next, Steve Carlton leads his fellow ROTC Cadets in their full Rifle Corp uniforms, swinging their hopefully unloaded weapons in what is supposed to be a show of skilled precision and military might. If we perform on the football field today like these guys are performing right now, we'll lose by sixty points. Mayor Seymour Denton marches in front of the last vehicle in the parade, a convertible Cadillac carrying the 1970 Grand Marshall Heavy Metal Mike McIntrye, the Pulverizing Pioneer from the class of

'48.

My dad and mom sit in the back seat. Dad has a dazed look in his eyes. I can tell this is not one of his better days. I can see Mom's lips telling him to "Keep waving, keep smiling." The people watching on the sidewalk are not sure whether to applaud or stare. I have no idea why my mother thought it would be a good idea to have Dad as the Grand Marshall of this year's homecoming—a very bad decision in my mind. In the past few years, Dad has been getting worse and worse. He very seldom speaks, getting up out of his wheelchair takes forever, and even the simplest tasks are impossible for him to accomplish. It's very hard watching what has happened to my dad. My personal coach from before I can remember, now scribbles down his words of advice, and hands them to my mother who has no problem picking up this torch. I miss my dad; I really do.

There were two reasons I came to Pioneer U to play football. One was to be a big fish in a small pond. The second was because my dad went here. He was the first Pioneer to be named All American. I've seen the films over and over of Dad on the gridiron. Nobody was tougher, nobody hit harder, and nobody was more tenacious on defense than Iron Mike McIntyre. When he hit you, you knew you'd been hit. After college, he was drafted by the Chicago Bears and he and mom moved with their new baby, me, to the Windy City. Dad played weak side linebacker and in the first six games of his rookie season, he was tearing up the league. He hit one New York Giant running back so high and hard the guy flipped totally around and came down on his head, knocking him out, and out of the game. Rumor had it, from that play forward, Dad had a price on his head. Whoever took him out would receive a big bonus check. It happened three games later. An offensive tackle came off his position, stunted left, hit Dad low, wrapped his arms around him, and lifted him off his footing. The tight end came from the far side of the line at full speed, put his head down, and leveled his helmet into Dad's unprotected forehead. When Dad went down, the offensive tackle came down

41

on his left knee. They said you could hear the bone crack all the way into the first five rows. The offense got fifteen yards for unnecessary roughness. Dad got a life of debilitating physical pain and decreasing mental capability.

Mom was sitting in the Soldier Field stands, with me on her lap, when it happened. She, like Dad, has never been the same since.

The NFL gave Dad a lousy pension, and we moved back to the Northwest. Dad got a job coaching at a high school. In the first three years he took a perennial loser and had them playing for the state championship. I was eleven when Dad got offered the head coaching position at a Division 2 college in Washington. In three years Dad had the team winning its division. The remainder of his time, he spent coaching me. We spent hours on the field. I must have run a million wind sprints and threw two million passes. My fundamentals were so perfect and precise college quarterbacks would look to me as an example. I was the starting quarterback my freshman year in high school. I got my name in Sports Illustrated my sophomore year. In my junior year, the headaches started. Not mine, my dad's. Some days, he'd be so bad he'd curl up on the carpet and have to lie perfectly still to relieve the pain. Dizzy spells followed. Numbness in his extremities was next. He was falling apart from the inside out. It was painful for me to watch, but nowhere near as painful as what he was going through.

He never complained.

He had to quit coaching.

At home, he tries to do everything he can, but he can't do much. He's my Dad, but he's not the Dad I once had. I want to take the Pioneers to the Rose Bowl, be the next Joe Namath, win the Super Bowl, and make my Dad proud.

The last entry to pass the reviewing stand isn't in the parade, it merely follows the parade. It is an old, flatbed truck. On its front is a sign reading, *Back by Popular Demand*. The back and sides of the truck are plastered with pictures of me in action. And on the bed of the truck are the Alpha Taus, already drunk, chanting "Do it brother, Tony, do it."

What a bunch of idiots.

## CHAPTER 6

The score is 28-24, 4th quarter, 24 seconds left on the clock. We're losing.

Unbelievable.

The game has been a disaster. For three quarters, the offensive line has had blocking amnesia, the receivers' hands have turned to stone, and the only holes the running backs have found are where the ball falls after they fumble. Worst of all, Praytel has called one of the dumbest, unimaginative, boring games in the history of sports. I've thrown so many short, swing passes, I'm dizzy. And I've had to scramble so much, I've got more yards on the ground, than in the air.

It's a miracle the score is this close, and we're still in the game.

Unbelievable.

We have the ball on their thirty-six. It's third and nine. A field goal does us no good. We get into the end zone or the season is over. No Rose Bowl. I call "time out." I walk slowly to the sideline. I can feel the pressure from every fan in the stadium; it's like they are pissed at me because we're losing. That's bullshit. It's not my fault.

Praytel and Arthur meet me on the sideline.

"We got time for at least two more plays," Praytel tells me, as if this is news to me.

"I don't think so," I tell him.

"Don't think. Just get a first down."

"We have to go downfield, now."

"Run X 16, off tackle, left," Praytel tells me. "Get the first down and call time out."

"No."

"Run X 16, off tackle, left," he repeats loud enough for Northern to hear.

"That play hasn't worked all day."

"It will if you run it correctly."

"We have to open this up, set up five receivers—force them to cover one-on-one. Do something different."

"They'll drop four into deep coverage, dumbshit." Praytel gets right in my face. "You'll throw a brick out there, and the game will be over."

"They're going to smell another swing pass the moment we set up."

"You do as you're told, McIntyre. Run X 16 off tackle, left."

I step back, look into the stands and see my mom hold her notebook up. Dad is next to her in his wheelchair.

"Now, get your ass back into the damn game."

It's impossible to argue with an idiot. "Fine," I say to Praytel.

The official comes over to hurry us up. Arthur puts on his helmet and follows me back onto the field. He's mumbling. I'll assume he's praying.

In the huddle, I kneel down, and tell my team in no uncertain terms, "Here's what we're going to do." I draw out the play on Lester's gut, as I explain the formation, and what everyone is going to do.

Arthur says, "But Coach Praytel said to run…"

Lester cuts Arthur off with, "Fuck, God-damned Praytel."

"On two," I order, and clap to break the huddle.

The crowd rises to their feet. Northern's defense lines up tight, as if another blitz is coming, both their safeties drop back. As I call out "Ready," my flanker comes in motion, and lines up next to the tight end. Their cornerback comes across the field with him.

"Set."

Praytel sees the shift and screams out, "What the hell are you doing?"

"Hut, hut."

The ball is snapped. I drop back, wait for my left end to break into the middle, and take the free safety with him. I turn in the opposite direction, jute the blitzing left-side linebacker. I step up in the pocket, look up field, pump fake, swivel right, and pass a lateral across and behind me to Arthur, breaking right. The defense immediately converges to stop the sweep. They've seen this play twelve times today. It shouldn't be too hard for them to figure out. I move left, slowly, making sure I'm on the outside of their defensive end. As Arthur approaches the line of scrimmage, he stops. I take off. Arthur lofts a pass across the field to the empty flat where I'm hitting full stride. I catch the ball, tuck it under my arm, and sprint downfield. Twenty yards in, Lester throws a devastating block on their cornerback. I cut to the middle, and then back left. I got one more guy to beat, which I do with a head fake. There's nobody around me. I'm cruising in for the score, the crowd's reaction is deafening. And, one foot from the touchdown line, I stop dead in my tracks. The crowd goes from a screaming frenzy into silent, absolute shock. Three of their defenders are sprinting towards me. I wait until the last possible second ticks off the clock before I dive into the end zone and score.

The gun sounds. Pioneers win. 30-28.

Pandemonium. I've never heard so much noise.

Lester comes over, scoops me off the ground, and lifts me onto his shoulders. The Pioneers on the field encircle us, jumping up and down, screaming and shouting. Our bench clears and runs towards us; the second and third string guys, who never get in the game, go the craziest. The band plays the fight song. The cheerleaders jump for joy. The students and fans pile out of the stands and onto the field. Praytel goes bananas, hugging and slapping the assistant coaches like this was all his doing. It's amazing how quickly Praytel can go from being an angry asshole to jubilant victor. The only person on the field not in a state of ecstasy is Arthur, who is on one knee, hands folded, looking to the sky, mumbling away. By the time the rest of the team joins the delirious scrum on the field, the city cops and stadium security give up on trying to maintain order. Nothing, or no one, can stop this celebration. Lester won't let me down. I take off my helmet

46

and pump my hands into the air in a victory salute of epic proportion. A perfect photo opportunity for the sports pages tomorrow and tonight's "Film at Eleven." My heart is beating faster than it did during the game.

The goal posts come down. People are hugging, kissing, and dousing each other with beer and liquor. Women are getting manhandled, but don't seem to care. I'm totally surrounded. Guys and girls try to break through to touch, but can't quite make it through the layers of football flesh protecting me. Everybody always wants a piece of the hero. I can't say I blame them. Looking across the sea of collegiate bodies, I can't pick out my frat brothers, but I can hear the chant, "Tony, Tony, Tony." The brothers are in the melee somewhere, squirting their boda bags of ouzo at each other, or copping a feel from some cheering, unsuspecting chick.

This is what football is all about. I love it. I want to do this the rest of my life.

By the time we get to the locker room, it is over-flowing with people. I don't get the chance to drop my helmet at my locker. The other players are tearing off their jerseys and pads, still bumping each other in triumphant revelry.

I'm pushed into the adjacent room and up onto the stage, in front of six or seven microphone stands. The lights from the TV cameras shine in my eyes. It's hard to see, but I have no problem hearing the first question asked by jerk-off, TV rat, Ace Dunnigan. "Was it your play or Praytel's that won the game?"

"What difference does it make?" I answer. "We won."

A landslide of questions follow.

"Why'd you stop on the one before taking it in for the score?"

"I wanted to see how many hearts would stop beating in the stands, as well as run off enough time on the clock so they wouldn't get the ball back, even on the kickoff."

"How hard was it to have Arthur pass the ball downfield, instead of you?"

"If anyone is blessed with a good arm, it's Arthur."

"Do you consider this your finest hour as a Pioneer?"

"The way I see it, my finest hour is always going to be in the next game I play."

My heart is still pounding. I'm pumped. It's like I never left the field.

The questions keep coming, faster than Northern's front four during the game. I do my best to give standard, cliché answers. "The only thing I think about is winning." "I play them one game at a time." "You take the step, when it is time to step up."

"Next week, it's the annual Civil War Game, second oldest rivalry in college football, you going to do to the Woodchucks what you just did to Northern?"

"As I told you before, I make touchdowns, not predictions."

With all the questions and commotion in the room, I don't see a scruffy, long-haired hippie make his way to the edge of the stage. And when a question is asked from the far right side of the room, I don't notice as the guy jumps up on the stage, and gets behind the microphones. But I do hear him scream out, "There's going to be something a lot more important than football next Saturday. We're staging a major rally on campus to let the politicians know we want out of Vietnam and out of Vietnam now."

The boos and catcalls from the crowd start at once. I'm a little short on the uptake, I just look at the guy and wonder, *What the hell are you doing?*

"Instead of screaming for touchdowns, it's time we all started screaming for peace."

"What?"

"What's important next Saturday..."

My left hand goes out and grabs the guy by his ugly, tie-dyed t-shirt. I pull him away from the microphone, "Shut the fuck up, buddy." I say out of media earshot.

"Tony, listen..."

"No."

He sweeps my hand off his chest, pushes back toward the

microphones, and raises his voice over the crowd, "Next Saturday..."

It doesn't take much to yank him away from the microphones; the guy's a wimp. I get a firm grip on his arm. I pull him towards me and he starts to put up a fight. Dumb. Now, I grab him with both hands, straighten him up, and throw him off the stage into the first row of folding chairs. He goes down like a split end blindsided by a free safety.

The next words I speak are to the intruder, but I make sure they go right into the microphones, "Next Saturday, buddy, there's nothing more important around here than football."

---

My mother picks the worst possible restaurant to have dinner. It's some hole-in-the-wall place on the outskirts of town. There is no ramp in the front, so I have to yank Dad in his wheelchair up six steps to get in the front door. Inside, it's dark, dank, crummy, and empty. I want to be at some packed place filled with a bunch of delirious Pioneer drunks reliving the victory over and over.

"What are we doing here, Mom?"

"I wanted a place where we could talk."

"Why?"

She leads us to the back of the place, to a red leather booth. As I pull Dad up to the aisle edge of the table, he reaches up with his better arm, touches me on my wrist, and pulls me down to him. With about all the energy he has left, after this very exhausting weekend, he whispers to me, "You did good."

"Thanks Dad."

I sit on the left side of the booth, next to Dad. Mom scoots in the other side and slides her way to the center; this is odd. And, as if on cue, she says, "Well, look who's here."

A short, dumpy, bald guy slides into the booth next to Mom, and across from me. He puts his left hand on Dad's upper arm, and says with a phony smile, "Heavy Metal, you're looking better all the time."

The guy wears a diamond ring on his pinky finger.

"Tony, you remember Justice, don't you?" Mom asks me.

Arnold "Justice" Segalman is from New York City. I'm told he's the slimiest, crudest, ball-busting, sports agent in the business. He lies, cheats, insults, makes absurd demands, goes back on his word, and sucks every dime possible from team owners, who hate negotiating with him. "Exactly the kind of guy you want on your side," my mother tells me. Justice has been after me since I was a freshman. Agents are not allowed to contact athletes while they are still in school, so he calls my mother, father, ex-coaches, anyone who he might suspect I'd go to for advice. He never lets up. He's an asshole. I don't like him, but maybe that's a good thing.

"I don't think I'm supposed to be talking to agents," I say to him.

"Tony," Mom says, "be polite."

"You looked good out there today, kid," Justice tells me. "Your team stunk, but you looked great. Not only can you throw, but you proved you had legs today."

"My son can do it all," Mom assures Justice.

"You know what I was seeing on the field today?" Justice asks me.

"No."

"I was seeing the next Joe Namath."

I don't comment, but I agree with him.

"You're only missing one thing," Justice says.

I can't imagine what it could be. "What?" I ask.

"Exposure."

"You can't go anywhere in this town without seeing my face," I tell him.

"Forget about this cow town, Tony," he says. "You have to play on a much bigger field."

"Okay," I say, not knowing what else to say.

Justice continues, "I want to let you know that people are going to get to know Touchdown Tony McIntyre a lot better in the next few weeks."

"Especially if he goes to the Rose Bowl," Mom adds.

"Even if that doesn't happen," Justice says. "I've pulled a few strings, and Tony McIntyre is going to be front and center in the eyes of America. Trust me."

Trusting this guy would be like trusting Praytel to call a good game.

"Even if we don't go to the Rose Bowl this year, I'll take them there next year," I say to him.

Justice sits back in the booth. He spins the ring around his pinky finger a few times. "Well," he says, "since you mentioned next year, you might be interested to know that there are three NFL teams with dire needs at quarterback. And there is no senior going into the draft who can throw a spiral equal to Touchdown Tony." Justice pauses for maximum effect. "Now, I don't know if a signing bonus would make you consider blowing off your senior year, but in my business timing is everything."

"How much of a signing bonus?" I have to ask.

"Five-hundred grand."

"That's all?" Mom asks.

"You blow the Woodchucks off the field next Saturday and the sky will be the limit, kid."

**CHAPTER 7**

The California schools lost. I have a real shot at the Rose Bowl. All I have to do is win next week.

You can't go anywhere on campus without seeing a sign or poster reading *Beat State, Wipe out the Woodchucks,* or *Go Pioneers.* Monday's Daily Pioneer's headline is *Un-Civil War Saturday.* Students wear green and gold. Both TV stations are doing specials this week. The statue of the Pioneer Mother in the middle of the quad sports a Pioneer football jersey. Sports reporters roam the campus looking for stories. The picture of me on Lester's shoulders, arms raised in victory, is everywhere; in the newspapers, store windows, gas stations, taverns, and neighborhood markets. My forty-foot banners hang again from the walls of the student union. There is a rumor that ABC might broadcast the game live to the entire country. A dead woodchuck, dressed as a farmer, hangs in effigy from one of the dorms. But by far, without a doubt, the best thing that happens is my picture is on the cover of Sports Illustrated. The headline reads, *Tony McIntyre, the Passing Pioneer.*

I guess Justice wasn't bullshitting after all.

The entire university is in Pioneer football hysteria.

The only other thing some people talk about is this peace march scheduled Saturday before the game. This march shouldn't be allowed. The peace-freaks are only doing this to take advantage of the crowds, which will be here for the game. It isn't fair. They should make these idiots walk someplace else. They should have to get their own publicity, and not be able to back onto ours. What really pisses me off is, you'll see the poster of me on Lester's shoulders, and some idiot has plastered a sticker reading, *Football at 3. Peace March at noon.* To believe a whole lot of hippie protestors walking in this town is going to make a difference in Washington D.C., is really ridiculous. There's been a ton of these marches at other colleges and universities, and they haven't made much of a difference. I didn't hear of any votes in Congress changing after those happened. I wish the whole march thing would go away, and we could just play football.

---

Shelly, yes, I remember her name, isn't in class on Monday, so I don't have much to look at. Ringly goes on and on about Macbeth, the witches, Shakespeare, what it all means or is supposed to mean. It's pretty boring. At the end of the class, he passes back our essays.

"No assignment this week," he tells the class. "With all that's going on around here, you probably wouldn't do one anyway."

The bell rings. Every student is reading over their grade and any comments Ringly made on their papers, except me. Once they leave the room, Ringly hands me my essay.

A red "F" is on the top of the page.

"I certainly hope you do better Saturday than you did on this paper," he says to me with a snarky grin.

I take another look at the grade, think what a bitch Shelly is, look up at the professor, and say, "Like I care."

I crumble up my essay, toss it into a trashcan six feet away, swish, and leave the room.

I have some time before lunch, so I head over to the student union.

The student union building is built in a half-circle. One side is all glass windows that face west, out to the stage where we had the rally the other day. Inside, there is a huge, common area where you can eat, drink, try to study, but mostly waste time between classes. It is supposed to be the spot on campus where all the different types of people going to Pioneer U can mix and mingle; learn about each other's cultures, differences, religion, politics, whatever, but this never happens. The whites hang out with the whites, the blacks with the blacks, the Asians with the other slant eyes, fat girls with fat girls, and losers with other losers. So much for diversity. People want to be with people like themselves. What's the matter with that?

Along the back end of the building, there is a long corridor with offices for the student organizations on campus. I have to walk through this hallway to get to my mailbox. On the door of the Black Student Union is a poster of those two Olympic runners who raised their fists when they were on the podium to get their medals. I always thought they were really stupid. After their stunt, there was no way they were ever going to get any endorsement money for track shoes or jock straps.  There is a picture of that Ché guy on the door where the Mexicans sit around and do nothing. And, if it was up to me, I'd put Bruce Lee, instead of Buddha, on the gook's door.

The biggest office is the one, right before the mailboxes. It's the office of the SDS. I'm not sure what the initials stand for, but it should be Stinky Dirty Students because everyone in the room is long-haired, greasy, and has dirt under their fingernails. Most have holes in their faded jeans and wear t-shirts with phrases like *Make Love, not War, End the War NOW*, and *Hell No, We Won't Go*. As I pass by, I can see the place is packed. There's all kind of activity going on. Rock music's playing way too loud. People are running off stuff on the mimeograph machines. Girls are painting posters. People sit at a long table and stuff envelopes. You can't miss smelling the marijuana smoke; it hangs over the room like a cloud. I bet a lot of these people aren't even students. If it was up to me, campus security would be at the door checking student ID's, like at a tavern where you don't get in without proper ID, or a phony one like I have. It only seems fair.

When I got to the U as a freshman, Mr. Swallow, the guy who recruited me, told me I'd be getting all my mail at student mailbox number 1174. He gave me the combination, which opens the cubbyhole, and told me it would be my official address at Pioneer U. I check the box about once a week. It's always filled. I get lots of letters from people and businesses asking me to do something for them, such as show up at their stores, attend their club meetings, visit their sick kid, or become a member of their lodge. I throw all these away. I get stuff from school, notices, schedules, stuff from my counselor, who I've never met, grades, test scores, whatever; most of these I throw in the trash too. Then there are ads for stuff I either get free or have no interest in buying. Sometimes, when I'm busy, and know there is going to be nothing important in the box, I take it all out, and toss it away without opening a single envelope.

I stand in front of my box today, fumbling with the little lock, when I see Marcus and cute, little Katie about to go into the SDS office with another guy and funky looking chick. "Marcus," I call out to get his attention.

He doesn't look up. He's talking a mile-a-minute to this guy. I can hear their conversation.

"A bunch of George Wallaces live in this town?" The guy asks Marcus.

"Enough."

"This town is like a knot on the John Birch tree."

"I like it here," the chick says. "I bet Beaver Cleaver lives right between Father Knows Best and Donna Read."

"Marcus," I try again, this time walking toward him.

He sees me when I'm a few feet away. He gives me a look, as if he doesn't want to be bothered, but that doesn't stop me.

"Hey, you're going to have to talk to that Shakespeare teacher of mine. He's being a real pain in the ass."

Marcus doesn't respond.

"Hi, Tony," Katie's polite enough to greet me.

"Hey, Katie, you're looking good."

I've never seen the guy next to Marcus. He's short, white, out of shape, with long, frizzy hair, and wears big sunglasses, probably to hide his bloodshot eyes. He's got a cigarette hanging in his lips, which he inhales without taking it out of his mouth. My first impression is the guy's a dick. The funky girl with him is cute in a weird sort of way. She looks about eighteen, but I can tell this chick has got a lot of miles on her—been around a lot of blocks, in not a lot of time; usually girls like this are great in the sack.

"Tony, I can't talk right now," Marcus tells me.

"Who're your friends?" I ask.

Reluctantly, Marcus says, "This is Hayden and Molly."

"I'm Tony McIntyre," I don't offer my hand to shake in fear I could pick up some disease from the slimy guy.

"They're here to help out with the march this weekend," Marcus explains.

"I've seen you somewhere," Molly says.

"I'm on the cover of SI this week."

"What's SI?" she asks.

"Sports Illustrated."

"No," she says. "I've never read that."

"I was in Newsweek last month," Hayden says. "Article about the takeover at Columbia."

I have no clue what the slime-ball is talking about.

"So, you're the big man on campus football star?" Molly asks me.

"Most people think so," I answer honestly.

"Why don't you march with us?" Hayden asks.

"March where?"

"The peace march before the game on Saturday, Tony," Marcus says.

"Yeah," Katie says, "that would be groovy if you marched with us."

"Saturday?" I can't believe what they're asking.

"It's going to be the biggest blowout this town has ever seen," Hayden says.

"Saturday's the Civil War game," I inform the idiots.

"The game's at three. The march is at noon." Marcus says. "Would you do it?"

"You're kidding, right?" I ask in disbelief.

"A lot of people would join in if Tony McIntyre marched," Katie says.

"We're marching for peace, to get us out of an unjust war,

and bring the troops home," Molly, the hippie chick, says.

"The only place I'm marching on Saturday is down the football field, as many times as I can," I tell them.

"Then make a statement to the press," Marcus says.

"If I go mouthing off to the press, it'll only fire up the Woodchucks." Don't these people know anything?

"Make a statement to the press on how you support the peace movement," Marcus says.

"What are you people smoking?"

"Hash," Hayden says.

I shake my head back and forth, as if this conversation has come out of the Twilight Zone. "I don't know anything about the war or what you people are trying to do. And I don't care."

"You have to care," Molly says.

"No, I don't. All I care about, and all anybody else is going to care about on Saturday, is if I take this team to the Rose Bowl."

"So, you won't make a statement?" Katie asks as if she hasn't heard a word I've said.

"No, I won't."

"How about if you got stoned with us, right out in the open, let the press take pictures. That would really make a statement," Hayden says. "And they'd never arrest the big man on campus right before the big game. It would be totally righteous."

"You people are out of your minds."

Marcus is embarrassed. I can tell he wants this all to end. "I'll see you at the regular time."

"I'm not going back to that library," I tell him.

"Fine."

I win again. Maybe I should be the tutor, and he should be the student.

I reach over to touch Katie before I walk away. The Molly girl gives me a strange smile as Hayden lights up another cigarette with the tip of the one that's still burning. Once he inhales a big puff from the new one, he drops the old butt on the floor and grinds it out into the carpet.

"If you change your mind, let me know, okay?" The Molly girl says before I'm out of earshot.

"Yeah, that's going to happen."

On my way to my mailbox, two girls come up, and one asks, "Would you sign your picture for me, Tony?"

"Sure." I wait for her to find a pen and hand it to me along with the Sports Illustrated. She's not bad looking. "What's your name?"

"Mary."

I give her my Tony smile, and watch her turn a little red. This is where, if she looks like she's worth it, I ask for her phone number, but this time I don't get the chance.

"But it's not for me," she says. "It's for my dad."

"What's his name?"

"George."

I write his name on the top of the cover, *Rose Bowl here I come* beneath it, sign my name, twice as big as the other letters, and hand it back to Mary.

She giggles as she says, "Thanks."

I'm not big on girls who giggle, so I merely turn back to my mailbox. The two walk away, giggling together.

The mailbox is stuffed. I have to wedge the papers and envelopes out carefully. Once I have them stacked in my hand, I rifle through, pull out the over-sized ads, and let them fall to the floor. I zip through the smaller stack, and find a white envelope, addressed to me with no return in the upper left corner. I tear open the letter, pull out one folded blank sheet, unfold it, and remove the five $20 bills inside. I stuff them in my pocket. I got what I came for.

There are six or seven letters left. One is from a sporting goods store in town wanting me to sign autographs for their new store opening in February. There's one from a company who wants to talk to me about a stock portfolio, whatever that is. The next two are obviously junk, and I don't bother opening either. Another is from the U, something about my transcripts; I'll save this one for Marcus. The last is different than any I've ever received. My name isn't written or typed on the front, but printed from some mailing machine.  The return address is three capital letters with Washington D.C. beneath it. I open the envelope and take out the one page. There is the date, my name, Mr. Anthony McIntyre, and my P.O. Box address. The letter begins with the word:

*Greetings,*

## CHAPTER 8

This has to be a mistake.

The letter says I have to report for a physical in two weeks. I don't need a physical. I'm on the cover of Sports Illustrated. I'm in the running for the Heisman Trophy, and I could go to the Rose Bowl. Why the hell would someone think I need a physical? Somebody screwed up, and somebody screwed up big time.

How could I get drafted? I have a student deferment. My mother made sure I had one of those. It's the law. The government doesn't take students to become soldiers, they take the colored guys from the ghettos, and the white guys who don't graduate from high school; that's who goes in the Army, not guys in college like me.

This has got to be a mistake. There is no way this can be happening to me.

I lean against the wall of mailboxes and try to think this through. All I can come up with is Steve's in ROTC, he'll know what to do. I cram the letter in my pocket with the money and the transcript notice, lock up my mailbox, and hustle down the hallway.

Outside the student union, Marcus and his protestor buddies are in the middle of the street. The traffic has stopped. A couple of the hippies pound on drums, three slap their tambourines, and a few sing protest songs. There must be thirty people, including Hayden and Molly, passing out fliers advertising the march on Saturday, and hundreds of people milling around in the middle of the road. The two campus security guards on duty give up trying to clear the hippies, and stand at the two street intersections rerouting the cars in other directions. It is quite the scene.

I could care less. I just want to get back to the house and talk to Steve.

And suddenly, there's an ear-splitting roar, which almost knocks me off my feet. At least eight motorcycles ride into the street belching gas fumes, busting eardrums, and scattering the crowd in a million directions. The gang, dressed in black leather jackets, Nazi-stomper boots, and heavy chains dangling from their necks or waists, tear down the street at at least forty miles per hour. When they screech to a halt at the end, they half-spin around, and roar back the way they came. Some do wheelies; some take out pedestrians. They rev their engines so loud, it is impossible to hear the screams of fear in the crowd. They never get off their bikes. They just keep driving up and down the street, scaring the hell out of everyone.

I hightail it back up the steps of the student union, where I know they can't get me. I see protestors trapped in the middle of the street, petrified, not able to move in any direction for the fear of being hit by a Harley. Marcus and Katie are perfect targets in the middle of the street. He's spit on at least three times that I see. Up the street, Molly grabs a crying, frantic young girl, dodges the bikes to the sidewalk, and finds safety for the girl behind a pine tree. Hayden doesn't waste a second before running out of the street, up the block, and into the Pioneer Cemetery a couple hundred yards away. Panic is the last name of this protester.

Police sirens are heard in the background, and the motorcycles speed off as fast as they came. The whole thing ends as quickly as it began. Only the thick smells of gasoline and exhaust remain in the air. Hundreds of the fliers that were being passed out were dropped in the confusion, and now become trash, littering the campus, as they blow freely in the wind. What a mess.

I get myself the hell out of there. I've got more important things to deal with.

It's a little past eleven when I get to the house. Steve is not in his room. I go down to the kitchen to check there. Ruthie is busy making soup of some kind.

"Steve here?"

"Lunch isn't for a half-hour."

I'm about to turn and leave the room.

"You never have any books," Ruthie says to me.

"What?"

"You're a student, but you never have any books."

"So?"

"Jerry wasn't a very good student, but he always carried his books."

"Jerry wasn't on his way to the NFL," I explain to her.

"When he gets out of the Army, he promised me he'd go back to college, but he'll need books."

"He can have mine."

Ruthie moves from the edge of the stove, comes over to me, and places her hand on my forehead. "Are you sick?"

"No."

"You look sick."

"I'm not."

Her hand pushes against my face. "You don't have a fever." She won't let go. "Is it from not getting enough protein?"

"No." I reach up and remove her hand. "Somebody screwed up and now I got to fix it."

"Can I help?"

"No."

I go up to my room, lie on my bed for a few minutes, but can't relax. I'm nervous, jumpy, and pissed off. I get up, grab my car keys, and go to the back of the house where my car is parked. The Firebird is not really my car, but a loaner I get to use while I'm in school. I fire it up, back out into the alley, and take off for downtown.

Six blocks later, I glance in my rearview mirror and see red and blue lights flashing behind me. Damn. I pull over. I roll down my window, and wait for the cop, carrying his ticket book, to approach my window.

"In a hurry?" he asks.

"Yeah, I am."

The cop backs up, takes a longer look at me, and says, "You're Touchdown Tony."

"What can I do for you?"

I sign a copy of my Sports Illustrated, promise I'll send his kid an autographed football, and get off with a "watch your speed on city streets" warning.

Fair trade.

I let him leave before I get back on the road.

I've been by this place before. It's right near the movie theater on Pine Street. I slow up to see a whole bunch of people come out of the theater. *Easy Rider* is playing. I've never heard of it. I go up the street, make a U-turn at the light, come back the other way, and see the building on my right. No wonder I didn't see it, there's a whole slew of people out front, walking back and forth, crowding up the sidewalk.

There's no place to park in the front, so I go around the back. The parking lot is full. I'm in a hurry. I park in a red zone. I have to walk all the way around to the front, because there is no back entrance. I push through the protestors, who are now chanting "Give peace a chance." One of them recognizes me and shouts out, "Hey, Touchdown Tony." Another one asks, "Can I have your autograph?" I blow by all of them and into the building.

It's one big room, painted a depressing shade of grey. Army, Navy and Marine posters are the only decorations on the walls, unless you include the crooked picture of Richard Nixon. In the front of the room is one long, high counter. Six or seven clerks, all wearing short-sleeved shirts and thin ties, sit on high chairs; some have lines of guys waiting to talk to them. One has a sign that reads "Closed". I go to that guy. I hand him the letter. He doesn't read it.

"You're Touchdown Tony."

"This is a mistake," I tell him slapping the letter with my finger.

"I'm counting on you to beat the spread this weekend," he tells me.

"They sent this to the wrong person," I try to explain.

"State's got a weak safety, and a weaker left cornerback. If you open it up and throw downfield, you'll pick 'em apart."

"Fine, I'll do that," I assure him. "This is a mistake." I point at the letter again.

He finally reads, then asks, "What's your number?"

"Twelve."

"Not your number, number, your draft number?"

"I don't know."

"You taking a full load?"

"Yes."

"Flunk any?"

"What?"

"You pass fifteen units last quarter?"

"I think so."

"You don't pass fifteen units, you lose your deferment," he says.

"How the hell would they know that?"

"They get your transcripts."

This is all news to me. "I got to get this fixed. I can't get drafted by the Army."

"You already have."

"I'm getting drafted by the NFL."

"They're going to have to wait their turn." This clerk is being a real ass.

"I ain't taking this shit," I tell him.

"Unless you flunk your physical, your raft of shit is just beginning."

I pull the letter back. "It's a mistake. You have to do something about this."

"Who do I look like, Robert McNamara?"

I turn away from the jerk, re-stuff the letter into my back pocket, and hear him say, "And, no matter what Praytel calls, throw it downfield."

---

I find Steve in the ROTC office, which is what used to be a tool shed near the athletic fields. On the door, people have spray painted the words: *Pigs, Murderers,* and *Baby Killers*. He sits behind a small desk. There's the same picture of Nixon I saw at the draft board office on Steve's wall. His hangs crooked too. It's freezing in this dumpy, little room.

"First thing you have to do is find out why you didn't get 15 units," Steve says after handing the letter back to me.

"How do I find that out?"

"It's got to be on your transcript."

I dig into my back pocket for the other letter I got in the mail, but I must have left it in my room. "Then what should I do?" I ask.

"Talk to the teacher."

"And if that doesn't work?" I'm trying to think ahead.

"I don't know."

"You got to know. You're in the military."

"I do know you shouldn't tell anyone about this," he says. "The more people know, the harder it's going to be to get out of."

He's right. I better shut up.

Steve looks up at the clock on the wall. "Aren't you late for practice?"

Now Praytel is going to be on my ass too. I hurry out of the crummy office. "Pick me up after practice."

"I can't. I got to see Cindy. The Candle Passing's this week."

I don't know what he is talking about, and I don't care. All I care about is fixing this problem.

"Hey, wait," Steve says before I leave. "I know what to do. Go see your sponsor. Swallow is wired into everybody in this town. He'll be able to help."

---

"What are you doing McIntyre?" Praytel is on me like stink on shit.

And deservedly so. My head is so far out of this practice that I might as well be in my room tossing my tennis ball against the wall.

65

"Sorry."

"If it's an out pattern, you might want to consider throwing the ball to the outside," Praytel says.

"Maybe if I was throwing the ball downfield, more than ten yards each time, I could concentrate on what I'm doing a lot better," I say more as an aside than a shot right back at him.

My inflection doesn't matter. Praytel comes at me, grabs me by the facemask, pulls me to his rotten breath, and screams, "You got lucky once, McIntyre, don't be thinking you're going to get lucky again, because you won't."

"I was just saying..."

He cuts me off. "You don't be saying and you don't be thinking," He wails. "All I want you doing is doing. Doing what I say, when I say it. You got that McIntyre?" He gives me one last jerk of my helmet to drive his point home. "Run the play and run it 'til you get it right."

Now, I'm pissed. My head is starting to throb.

Arthur takes my arm and pulls me away from Praytel. "Tony, don't. Just let it go."

"I'm getting real tired of turning the other cheek with this asshole, Arthur."

"Keep it on the field, Tony. You got to keep it on the field," Arthur is doing his best to calm me down.

The next ball I throw is a perfect, eight-yard spiral on the outside shoulder of the down-and-out right end. You can't throw a more perfect pass.

The remainder of the practice is awful. So many thoughts go through my brain, my head feels like it's going to bust open. I can't concentrate. I forget plays. I move to the wrong side. I trip setting up. Praytel's screams, echoing inside my helmet, make it all the more painful. We go over and over the same dumb plays; running one after another, after another. When the whistle finally blows to end the agony/practice, I'm exhausted.

"May I remind you, McIntyre, the biggest game of your life is this Saturday," Praytel says as he walks beside me into the locker room. "You might want to consider taking it seriously."

I want to take off my helmet and slam it into his face, but I don't have the energy.

---

I find the transcript on the floor of my room. Last quarter I got a B, two C's, a D, and an I. What's an I?

I have to read the entire page to find out an I stands for Incomplete. I can't remember any incomplete. The title of the course is Philosophy 101. Why would I ever take a course I can barely spell?

**CHAPTER 9**

My clock radio goes off at 9:15 am.

"The rumor you heard first, right here, is that Tony McIntyre is going to blow off his senior year at Pioneer U and go into the NFL draft this spring."

Yeah, just how I wanted to wake up after a miserable night's sleep to the voice of asshole Ace Dunnigan.

"The rumor, which has been substantiated by a number of my sources, had Tony, his dad Iron Mike, and his mother, Verna, having dinner with super-agent, Arnold "Justice" Segalman, in an out of the way restaurant, after Tony's last-second victory over Northern, last Saturday."

I fumble around to find the off switch, but can't; so I have to listen.

"If Tony doesn't take us to the Rose Bowl this year, getting there next year, without him, is virtually impossible. My NFL sources tell me if Tony does opt out of college and goes pro, he could demand a signing bonus in the Joe Namath category."

Enough. I unplug the radio.

I get up. Thirty minutes later, I'm on campus, standing outside Heady Hall. First period is almost over. I see someone I recognize, but she's not who I'm waiting for.

"What are you doing here?"

"What does it look like I'm doing here?" She's behind a small table with stacks of t-shirts lined up in a row. One is unfolded, on display. It reads: *Out of Vietnam, NOW.* "These are five dollars, the ones with two colors are six. Wanna buy one?"

"No."

"Wanna buy two?"

"Why are you doing this?" I ask.

"I enjoy eating," Molly says. "It's the way we make a living."

"You and Hayden?"

"Yep."

I turn to watch the students start to file out of the building. Class is over.

"What are you doing here?" Molly asks.

"Waiting to talk to somebody."

"Who?"

"Teacher."

Molly picks up a copy of the day's Daily Pioneer. The headline reads: *5000 to March on Saturday*. "You read about the march?"

"No."

"The original headline was going to be 500, but Hayden convinced them to add a zero."

I'm not looking at her. "Good for him." I'm watching the crowd, hoping to remember what the woman looked like.

"You're not much on current events, are you?" she asks.

"No."

I see her. She's walking my way. Now I remember.

"Got to go," I say to stop her.

She's old, well over forty. Short, small, wears a coat that goes all the way down to her ankles, and a pair of thick glasses, way too heavy for her nose. She should get contacts.

"Yes."

"I have to talk to you."

"Do I know you?" she asks.

"Spring quarter I was in your philosophy class."

"You don't look familiar." She gives me a weird squint through her coke-bottle lenses.

"Tony McIntyre."

"I don't remember you in my class," she tells me.

"You gave me an incomplete," I remind her.

"Okay."

"Why did you do that?" I ask.

"I don't know," she says. "Did you do the assignments?"

"I'm sure everything was handed in that was supposed to be handed in," I assure her.

"The only reason you would have received an incomplete is if

69

you didn't hand in the assignments or didn't take the final."

I pause. I remember. It was the end of spring practice; we went out drinking the night before, and I got wasted. I slept in the next day.

"Whatever," I tell her. "You have to go back and change the incomplete to a D."

"What?"

"You have to change my grade."

"And why would I do that?" She asks me.

"Because I have to have fifteen credits per term to keep my deferment."

"Yes."

"So, you have to change it."

"I can't do that."

"Yes, you can, Professor Warner."

"It's Wehner, not Warner."

Although it's a wet forty degrees out, I'm sweating under my parka. "Listen," I try to reason with her. "I'll get you four tickets on the fifty yard line for the Civil War game this Saturday."

"You're joking?"

"No."

"You want me to commit fraud for tickets to a football game?"

"They're worth at least fifty bucks a piece."

"I don't like football."

My voice is getting higher, but I can't help it. "It's the biggest game of the year."

"I don't care." She starts to walk away.

I stand in her path. "My transcript's got to say I completed fifteen units."

"You should have considered that fact before you neglected to take the final."

"You have to help me."

"No, I don't."

"Yes, you do," I shout back.

70

"Do you realize you're asking me to jeopardize my career?"

"Do you realize if you don't change it to a D, you'll be screwing the whole school, because I won't be taking the Pioneers to the Rose Bowl?"

"Who are you?"

"I'm Touchdown Tony McIntyre."

She pushes her glasses back up on her nose and says to me, "If you need a hand, Mr. McIntyre, I would suggest you look no further than your arm." She turns and hurries off.

I'm numb.

"Let me guess," I hear from behind me. "You were rehearsing for a play?"

I turn slightly to see Molly. "The bitch is screwing me," I tell her.

"Then I would suggest you relax and enjoy it."

## CHAPTER 10

I was a junior in high school. We're playing for the league championship, and we go in at the half up by three touchdowns. We come back on the field, and everything turns to shit. Our guy fumbles the kick-off; their guy picks it up for the score. We get the ball back. I throw downfield. My guy is wide open, and the ball bounces off his hands into the safety's hands for an interception. They do a trick play in their next series and score again. Now, we're only up by a score. We get the ball back. I toss one forty yards into the end zone, and it's called back for holding. I'm ready to shoot my offensive guard. Next play, I'm called for intentional grounding. Is the ref kidding or is he blind? We have to punt, and it's blocked. They score. The game's tied.

It's a game of Murray's, Murphy's, or Mallory's Law: *Everything that can go wrong, does; and it just doesn't stop.*

I'm in the middle of the Murray/Murphy/ Mallory's law right now. I hate it.

---

The Swallow Lumber Company is north of town, a little past where the river takes a big bend to go west. The place must be six blocks long. On one end there's a line of trucks, loaded with gigantic tree trunks, waiting for a fifty-foot crane to unload the logs. There are two other cranes, but these are at the edge of the river, where thousands of logs inside a big float thing, have been pulled by tugboats to the edge of the riverbank. The cranes pluck them out of the water and stacks them in plies going hundreds of feet into the air. The noise is deafening. The smell of diesel fumes in the air is nauseating. In the middle of the lumber operation is a building that stretches on forever. It's tall with a metal roof, no windows on either side, and open on the ends. Inside there are conveyor belts to bring the logs in, and huge circular machines

72

which strip off the bark. Massive saws cut the logs into smaller pieces, which are stacked near the far end of the building. If I thought the noise was bad outside where the cranes were working, it's nothing compared to the racket going on inside. I have the windows rolled up in the Firebird, and it's still so loud I can barely think.

What I should have done is kept on the main highway, all the way to the end of Swallow property, where the Swallow Inc. building is located; but I didn't know that. I've never been here before. It takes me a good twenty minutes to drive through the entire operation, dodging log trucks, bulldozers, pick-ups, and dump trucks. When I get to the building, I park in one of the empty "Reserved" spots, and hurry in the front door to get away from the noise and smell.

The lobby is really nice. And quiet. The receptionist sits beneath a sign reading: *American Lumber Keeps America Strong*.

"May I help you?"

"I'm here to see Mr. Eugene Swallow."

"Do you have an appointment?"

"No, he told me I could come out anytime I wanted."

"Your name?"

"Tony McIntyre."

The lady picks up her telephone, punches one of the buttons on the console, and says, "A Mr. Tony McIntyre is here to see Mr. Swallow." She listens, then asks me, "The football Tony McIntyre?"

"Yes."

"Have a seat. Someone will be right out."

I sit in a big leather chair. On the table there is only one magazine, *Lumberman's Weekly*. I never knew there was a magazine about lumber. I page through it, but it's mostly charts, graphs, and ads from companies in the lumber business. Pretty boring. I put it down after a couple of minutes. I'm getting fidgety. I wonder if I should tell the receptionist to tell Mr. Swallow I have to be at practice in an hour.

I try to get her attention, but she's too busy answering one phone call after another. Five more minutes go by. I'm just about ready to go up and talk to the receptionist again, when an older lady comes out a door to the left of where I came in.

"Mr. McIntyre?"

I stand up.

"You look taller on television."

She holds the door open for me to pass through, and then points for me to walk to the left.

I'm in another huge room. This one filled with small square workspaces. In each space there is a desk with a guy talking on the telephone. On the desk are long forms, which the guys fill out as they speak into the receiver. Younger guys run around the room picking up the completed forms, and delivering them to women seated at the edges of the room. These women take the forms, and transfer the information to other forms. The room is as loud as it is outside, but a different kind of loud. Outside is pounding, sawing, and crashing; while inside is ringing, screaming, and chattering. I'm not sure which is worse.

"Is Mr. Swallow expecting you?" the lady asks, as she leads me through the maze of salesmen, secretaries, and runners.

"No."

She leads me to the far back corner of the building. She stops at a desk where the phone is ringing, and picks it up. "He'll be right with you." She punches a red button on the bottom of her phone, then punches one of the buttons blinking. "He hasn't picked up yet?" She punches the red button again. She does this all with a calm ease, as if this is normal.

"Right this way."

I follow her down a short hallway and into the corner office.

Eugene Swallow is seated behind a desk, so big at least three trees lost their lives. He is smoking a cigar and screaming into the phone. "I'll take one cent off per board foot, and if he doesn't take it, you tell him the only two-by-four he's going to get from me is the one that goes up his ass."

The lady doesn't blink an eye.

Mr. Swallow slams the phone down, comes out from behind the desk, takes the cigar out of his mouth, and hugs me. Gross.

"Touchdown Tony, you're looking good, boy. You're looking good."

"Hello, Mr. Swallow."

The lady interrupts us. "Your wife is on three and Ginger is on four."

"Yeah, okay."

Mr. Swallow sits me down in one of the chairs, which face his desk, and backs up to lean against the front edge of his desk. He puffs on his cigar. "I've been hearing a lot about you in the last couple of days, Tony."

"Mr. Swallow, you said if I ever needed something…"

"Yeah?"

The lady repeats, "Wife on three."

"Get rid of my wife."

"Mr. Swallow, I got a problem."

He cuts me off. "You knock up some little doll baby, and need a little help?"

"No."

"I bet you get more ass than a toilet seat."

I remember what Steve told me, and I wait until the lady leaves the room. "Mr. Swallow, I got this letter from the draft board, somebody made a mistake…"

He cuts me off again. "The spread on the game is six points. Tony, I'm counting on you to beat that spread."

"Mr. Swallow, I need a favor…"

"And I need you to beat that spread."

The lady's voice comes out of the phone somehow. "Mr. Kisor is on six."

On his way back around the desk, he says, "Tony, let me give you a little advice. Do one thing at a time and do it right. You think I got where I am by fucking around with a bunch of shit every day? No, I do one thing at a time and get things done."

I am about to speak, but he picks up the phone.

"Bernie Kisor, how the hell are you?" A pause. "You know I'm trying to work with you, Bernie, but I can't keep this place open with the prices you want to pay." As Mr. Swallow listens, he puts up a finger to tell me he'll only be a minute. "If that's what Boise is willing to do, then I say 'go buy their knotty-ass, wormed-out wood.'" He listens. "Fine, you got to do what you got to do, Bernie."

Mr. Swallow hangs up the phone and says to me, "Guy's a lying sack of shit." He puffs on his cigar. "It's only six points, Tony. I'm not asking for the moon here."

"Mr. Swallow…"

The voice comes out of the phone again. "Your wife on three, wants to hold."

"Tony, you just worry about football. All that other shit we'll work out after you beat the spread. I promise." He puts the cigar back in his mouth, and his hand out to shake.

I stand and pump his fat paw. What else am I going to do?

Mr. Swallow picks up the phone, punches one of the blinking lights, and says, "Ginger, I bet you are looking good right now, real good."

**CHAPTER 11**

If I thought practice couldn't get any worse than the last time, I was wrong. Today is horrible.

One play I go left on a sweep right and slam face-to-face with Arthur. "Damn," he says, lying on the ground holding the sides of his skull. It's the first time I've ever heard him swear.

Another play, instead of my usual five-step drop back, I only make it 4 ½, and land on my butt. On an inside crossing pattern, I throw too soon, and the two ends collide. On an off-tackle run left, I wait too long to hand-off, and some third stringer comes through the line and nails me in the backfield. Can't this idiot see I'm wearing a red jersey? And you never tackle anyone wearing a red jersey!

The only positive about this practice is that it is taking years off Praytel's life. After every play he turns into a screaming, insane maniac. He's on me like sweat on a jock. He never lets up. He never stops. He gets worse and worse. This one vein on the side of his head is throbbing so fast and hard, it might explode, and all the blood will drain out of his little brain.

"What the hell is the matter with you, McIntyre?"

"I have to talk to you."

"About what?" he screams even louder.

I look around at my teammates before I say, "Alone."

"What?" Praytel must not have *alone* in his vocabulary.

"I have to talk to you alone."

"Well, whatever it is, it's going to have to wait, because if you think we're going into the game Saturday looking like you're looking right now, you must be high on love weed. Now run the damn play until you get it right." He blows the whistle loud enough to shatter glass.

I endure another twenty minutes of plays, fifty push-ups, and ten wind sprints. Praytel finally gives up, or he's too stupid to come up with any more punishment.

Ten minutes later, I'm sitting in Praytel's office. The door is closed, but I'm sure people are outside listening. The room is a square with cinderblock walls. It's cold, clammy, and smells like dirty sweat socks. I take off my wet jersey and sit shivering in my pads. My elbows are on my knees, and my hands are folded in front of me. Praytel's pacing back and forth behind his banged-up, metal desk.

"What in God's name are you doing out there?"

"Would you just listen to me?" I plead with him.

He stops, puts his hands on his hips, and faces me. "This better be good, McIntyre."

I can't look at him. I stare down to the linoleum floor. "I'm getting drafted."

"What?"

"I said, I'm getting drafted."

"Drafted by who?" he asks.

"The Army."

"What?"

"I screwed up. I didn't have enough units last quarter, and got a letter from the draft board telling me I have to report for my physical." There, I said it.

"You flunked out?"

I don't respond. What would be the point?

"Nobody flunks out of Pioneer U," he says incredulously. "We pick your classes. You get a tutor. All you have to do is show up." He leans on his desk towards me. "How in hell did you manage to flunk out of this place?"

"It was the last day of spring practice. We all went out drinking. I got hammered, slept in the next day, and missed this bullshit philosophy final I was supposed to take."

"No one could be that stupid, McIntyre."

I don't bother to respond for the second time.

Praytel starts to pace again.

"I tried to get the teacher to change the grade to a D, but the bitch wouldn't do it," I tell him.

"You want me to change your grade?" Praytel asks, then answers his own question, "I can't do that."

"I know."

"What do you want me to do?" he asks.

"Fix it."

"How?"

"I don't know."

"We have the biggest game of our lives this Saturday," he tells me, as if I don't know this already.

"And a week later, I have to report for my physical."

Praytel stops pacing, turns to me. "How could you be so stupid?"

"Look," I raise my head, and for the first time look him right in the eye. "I can't get drafted by no Army. I have an NFL career waiting for me."

As soon as the words come out of my mouth, I regret them. Praytel's expression changes from anger to absolute disdain. "So, it's true?" he says.

"No." I lie.

"You're going to blow us off and go into the NFL?"

"No."

"Don't lie to me, McIntyre."

My eyes go back to the linoleum.

"Then why don't you ask the NFL to help you?" He says in a snarky tone. Jerk.

It's quiet for a few moments. I want to cry, but I never cry. I don't think I know how.

He stops at his desk. "How many people know about this?"

"A couple."

"Don't tell anyone else," he says. "Not only will you look dumb as a goalpost, but if the team finds out, they'll lose every bit of confidence they might still have in you."

"I might be stupid, coach, but I'm not that stupid."

He sits in his desk chair, pushes some papers out of the way, and laces his fingers in front of him as if he might pray. "I'll see what I can do, McIntyre. In exchange, you keep your mind on football. We have to win on Saturday."

I stand up slowly and turn to leave the room.

"I really believed we could go undefeated next year," he says. "I guess I should quit considering the possibility."

I don't respond for the third and final time.

---

I'm back at the house before 5 pm. I'm not hungry, but I'm thirsty. I go into the kitchen. Ruthie is cooking up some disgusting looking stew, but tonight she's got competition. Three of the brothers, Ralph, Ernie, and Dudley are mixing up a revolting, smelly, rancid, disgusting concoction in the pot Ruthie uses to make soup. I listen to the boys as I get a glass of milk.

"Do you know how to stop a brother from getting tubbed?" Ralph asks Ernie.

"No."

"Good."

I ask, "What are you doing?"

Dudley answers, "Tonight, we try to disengage the engaged from being engaged to be engaged."

I could care less.

Ruthie is not happy sharing her kitchen. She says to me, "I didn't get a letter yet."

"Your kid's probably busy," I tell her, as if I know why her kid hasn't written. I've never written my mother a letter in my entire life, and probably never will.

I finish my milk and go upstairs to my room. I lie down on the small bed, and toss my tennis ball into the air. I have to think this out, but I can't figure out where to start.

I'm not sure how long I've laid here. I might have even fallen asleep, but I hear Steve come out of his room into the hallway near the stairway, and say to someone, "You got the right address?"

80

"Does Tony McIntyre live here?" Another voice, I faintly hear, asks in response.

"Yeah."

"Then I got the right address." I can hear him better. He must be on our floor. The voice is familiar.

"You some salesman or something?" Steve asks.

"No."

"Then why do you want him?"

"None of your business."

"Brother Tony is my business," Steve tells him.

"Maybe I'm here to shine his shoes," Marcus tells Steve.

I step out into the hall and see two other brothers standing with Steve. "What's going on?"

"I caught him sneaking around," Steve says.

"I wasn't sneaking around," Marcus says. "I was walking up your filthy stairway."

Steve and the brothers form a circle around Marcus. "You really think you're in the right place to be giving us shit, boy?"

"He's my tutor," I tell the bros.

"He don't look like a tutor," Steve says.

"He is."

Steve and the brothers part, and Marcus comes my way.

"And it's 'he *doesn't* look like a tutor,' not 'he *don't* look like a tutor.'" Marcus corrects the three.

Once we're in my room, I shut the door behind us.

"Nice friendly gauntlet you have to run to get in here." Marcus pulls off his backpack.

I lie back down on the bed and toss the tennis ball. Marcus pushes trophies and awards out of the way to make room for his stuff. "How'd you do on the Shakespeare paper?" he asks.

"What difference would it make?"

"That well, huh?"

Marcus unloads books from his bag. I toss the ball.

"Does everyone who gets drafted have to go to Vietnam?" I ask.

Marcus pauses at a question he never would expect to hear from me. "Yeah, it's another way to keep the brothers from rioting on the streets."

"What happens if you get drafted and you don't show up?"

Marcus gives me an odd glance. "They arrest you."

"Take you to jail?"

"Prison."

"Guy I know got drafted. He doesn't want to go."

"Can't blame him."

"He wants to get out of it."

"Can't blame him for that either."

"How do you get out of the draft?"

Marcus sits in the plastic desk chair and faces me. "Split to Canada, get caught robbing a liquor store, or flunk your physical."

"He can't do any of those."

"Is this a good friend of yours?" He asks.

I ignore his question and ask, "You're a senior, Marcus, what are you going to do when you graduate and get drafted?"

"I'm not getting drafted."

"Why not?"

"The only break this country's ever given me is a 302 draft number."

"You won't have to go?"

"Highly unlikely."

"I can't even remember what my draft number is." I admit.

"You're kidding."

"No," I tell him. "There always seems to be someone else around to worry about stuff like that for me."

"Must be nice."

"You know, I'm not really sure exactly where Vietnam is," I admit.

Marcus pulls a book out of his bag, *Vietnam, America's Nightmare* is on its cover. "It's in Southeast Asia. I'll leave this, and you can read all about it."

I pause. "Marcus, there's got to be another way of getting out of the draft."

"You can enlist in the National Guard or the Army Reserves, but that's one weekend a month for the next six hundred years of your life, plus two weeks every summer. And you still can get called up."

"How do you get into one of those?"

"The waiting line is as long as the Great Wall of China."

"How about if you knew somebody?"

"Maybe."

I pause to think this through and come up with one more question. "If you had a job where you had to work Sundays three months of the year, do you think the National Guard would let you switch to a weekday?"

"I doubt it."

## CHAPTER 12

The Delta House is two blocks away. I'm the last brother to arrive.

The sisters are in two lines across the front of the Georgian structure. Cindy, dressed in a white robe, stands on the steps, in the exact center between the two columns. There is a line of girls to her left and to her right. Steve stands behind her, a bit off to the side.

A candle passes from one girl to the other from the outside to the inside. The girls chant as the flame makes its way toward Cindy.

Oh Delta, Delta
Your candle lights the way
Through life's uncertainties,
Each and every day.
Oh Delta, Delta
Our hearts forever thine,
Allow your love to shine,
In sisterhood divine.

The two candles reach Cindy, who is bawling like a broken, pathetic loser, as the chant ends. She hands one candle to Steve and the other she raises like a priest raising his little pizza during a mass. Steve and Cindy blow out each other's candle simultaneously. The Delta sisters whimper and sniffle worse than if they're watching a movie where some kid dies in the end.

I'm standing way in the back. This is a total bunch of crap. I don't have time for this. I need to talk to Steve right away. I start to make my way forward, when the girls break their lines and converge on Cindy to whimper with her.

I am way too late getting to Steve. The brothers circle and move in fast. Steve sees them coming and tries to break free, but his escape doesn't work. Steve is tackled and piled on by four or five freshmen who obviously love pounding on an upperclassman.

One rips off his jacket. One rips off his shirt. Another brother takes a rope and ties his ankles. Ralph and Ernie each take an arm and yank a swearing Steve to a tree, where they tie him around the trunk like the Indians did to unlucky white men. Once Steve is securely fastened, his pants are stripped down to his knees. He's tied up tight with only his tighty-whities for protection.

"I'm going to kick the crap out of every one of you bastards." His threats don't mean much.

Dudley brings out the pot of slop, takes a ladleful, and dollops it on Steve's head.

Steve retches. The Deltas shriek in horror. One girl, Leslie, Linda, or Lucy, who must be the sorority president, is the only one who tries to stop the carnage. She screams at Dudley, "You are making a mockery of our candle passing ceremony."

Dudley tells her, "You got your rituals sister. We got ours."

"This is disgusting!"

"Hey," Dudley tells her and the rest of the Deltas. "It's the last opportunity for his brothers to shit on him before Cindy shits on him the rest of his life."

Dudley passes the ladle and each brother splatters a load of disgusting filth onto Steve.

"If there is any real shit in that, I will kick the shit out of every one of you bastards." Not now he won't.

Cindy, probably in fear of having her white robe end up a dirty napkin, flees the scene. "I can't bear to watch," are her final words before she splits into the house.

I'm the last in line to ladle, but I refuse. I bring a garden hose. "That's enough."

"But we haven't Tabasco sauced his nuts yet," Ralph informs me.

"Enough, I said."

I spray Steve down, wash the crap off of him, and out of his hair. I untie him. "Somebody get a blanket," I say to the girls, who have stood by watching the entire spectacle; most of them giggling at the absurdity of the situation. The brothers take off like cowards on a battlefield, running in all different directions.

"You better run you sons-of-bitches!" Steve screams.

"You know anyone in the National Guard?" I ask Steve.

"What?"

"You know anyone in the National Guard or Army Reserves?" I repeat the question.

"What are you talking about?" Steve raises his voice to me.

"You're in the ROTC; you got to know somebody."

Steve shivers as he stands in a puddle of slop.

"If you don't know, Diamond Jim will know, don't you think?"

The girl, who wraps a blanket around Steve, tells him, "We want this back."

"You have to take me to see Diamond Jim."

"When?"

"Now."

"Mind if I get showered and dressed first?" Steve spits the question at me.

"You have to hurry."

---

Steve grinds the gears of his Dodge Dart.

"If you get drafted, Tony, you got to go," Steve tells me. "It's the law."

"The only draft I'm going into is the NFL draft."

"You're declaring?" I don't see how he could be surprised.

"I'll go in the first round."

"We thought you'd take the Pioneers, undefeated, to the Rose Bowl next year?"

"My agent says I'll get the biggest signing bonus in history. Why go to the Rose Bowl when I can go to the Super Bowl."

Steve pulls into the American Legion parking lot. It must be bingo night or something, because it's after 10, and the lot is full. Diamond Jim's Deuce-and-a-Quarter is parked next to the front door. "Park behind him."

"It's not a spot."

"Just park the damn car, Steve."

Inside, forty- and fifty-something, white guys in both age and girth, are asshole to belly button with each other. It's not Bingo, but Nickel Beer Night. A cloud of cigarette smoke hangs in the place like a morning river fog and stinks to high heaven. Big round, glass ashtrays overflow with butts on the long cafeteria tables. Darts are flying. Two pool tables have six or seven quarters lined up on their felt edges. There is one small television set on a shelf over the bar. On the screen is a replay of me throwing the hippie off the stage after the Northern game. A big cheer goes up as the guy hits the deck. I listen to the legionnaires' comments: "If I woulda been there, I woulda kicked his ass right there." "If that were my kid, he'd be on the street after a stunt like that." "We make the world safe for democracy and this is the thanks we get?"

"Hey, you're Touchdown Tony."

I don't comment. I push through the crowd to where Diamond Jim teeters on a barstool.

"Tony, my man," Diamond slurs as he sees me approach.

"Diamond Jim..."

He's drunk, but he's not drunk enough to not notice Steve's not looking his usual self. "What the hell happened to you?"

"I was busy taking a lot of shit, standing up for your daughter," Steve tells him.

"Get used to it."

"Diamond Jim," I interrupt. "You know who runs the National Guard in town?"

"I know everybody."

"Would you call him for me?" I ask.

"Why?"

"Tony needs to talk to him," Steve says.

"I figured that," Diamond Jim replies.

"I just need to talk to him," I explain.

"Okay."

"Call him."

"Now?"

"I need to see him right away."

Diamond Jim gives me an odd, half-stewed, glance. His eyes are watery, face is pink, and the flesh hanging down under his chin looks swollen. "What's in it for me?" he asks.

"I'll see if I can score you a couple tickets for Saturday," I tell him.

"What do you mean 'see'?"

"Okay, I'll get you a couple seats."

"How about in the press box?" Diamond Jim slurs. "I heard they got free hot dogs and an open bar."

"Fine."

"I'll call and remind you to call in the morning," Steve tells him.

"That shit, I smell in your hair?" Diamond Jim asks his future son-in-law.

## CHAPTER 13

I can't sleep. I toss and turn about a thousand times. I stare at the ceiling. I look at the clock every minute. This is the first time I can remember lying in bed and not having sex, or not thinking about having sex. I have no idea what time I finally drifted off. I don't wake up until well after ten.

By the time I get downstairs to the kitchen, the breakfast stuff has been put away. It doesn't make any difference; I'm not hungry. I can see Ruthie get out of her car in the back and lug a couple of bags of groceries up the path to the back door of the house. I don't feel like having to talk with the cook this early in the morning, so I grab a glass of milk, and go out the swinging door that leads to the dining room and the front of the house.

The other brothers must be in class or still sleeping. I'm the only one downstairs. It's raining out, as usual. As I stand sipping my milk, I see a black sedan pull into the front driveway of the house. Two soldiers in fancy uniforms get out of the car, put on their shiny hats, and walk left, up the street, and out of my sight. I'm still standing in the same spot three minutes later when they return with another guy, who looks familiar. He's the priest from the Newman Center, four doors up, who comes over and complains we're making too much noise when he's trying to save souls or whatever. The two soldiers come in the front door.

"Is Ruth Babcock here?" the one with the most medals asks.

"She's in the kitchen."

"You're Touchdown Tony, aren't you?" the second soldier asks me.

"Yeah."

"Where's the kitchen?" the first guy asks.

I point. "What's going on?"

The two soldiers straighten their hats and push by me, followed by the priest.

"I'm Father Celcius."

I let them pass and follow through the dining room, but stop as they go through the swinging door.

Before the door stops swinging, I hear Ruthie scream, "No."

I rush into the kitchen. The two soldiers stand at attention, facing Ruthie. The first reads from a piece of paper in his hand. "We regret to inform you that your son, Jerry, has been killed in action."

I see Ruthie's knees actually buckle. She falls forward onto the kitchen counter, scattering vegetables, eggs, and other groceries to the floor. She's screaming "No!" over and over. Her face contorts into a frightening grimace that scares me. Father Cleon, Charley, or Cletus tries to catch her and hold her upright, but he can't do it. The soldiers do nothing to help. I push past them, grab half of the woman, and help her stand. Her screaming is relentless; she can't stop. She's impossible to hold. The priest is having a harder time than I am, trying to keep her upright.

The second soldier says, "Your son died bravely in the service of his country. You should be proud."

Father whoever grabs one of the kitchen lunch stools, pulls it over, and gets Ruthie to sit. I let go. I'm standing there, not knowing what to do or say. Ruthie has exhausted herself screaming and is crying uncontrollably.

The soldiers turn to leave the room. The second motions me to follow him out the door and into the dining room. There, we stop. The first one hands me the telegram, and the second adds the page he recited. "These are hers," the first guy says, and quickly turns to leave.

The second soldier follows, but as he passes me, he says, "I want you to be kicking some ass this Saturday, Tony." He gives me a slight punch to my shoulder and follows his buddy to their car.

I go back into the kitchen.

Ruthie remains on the stool, hysterical. She repeats phrases, over and over through her tears: "He was my only son." "This can't be happening." "He can't be dead, he can't be."

Father Priest does his best to comfort her, but he can't do

much.

I don't get too close. I can't for some reason. I stand back over by the spray sink and the dishwasher. I watch the woman literally age before my eyes. Lines form on her face, what muscle tone she might have had has disappeared, and she sags into a big lump of soft, mushy flesh. I step back as something comes over me. My head starts to pound, stomach turns, and sweat pours off my face. I can feel my teeth hurt. Ten seconds later, I double over, as if someone shoved a shovel blade into my gut. There is nothing but milk in my stomach. I retch repeatedly before it manages to escape out my mouth. From my hair to my toes, my whole body is convulsed in pain. All the times I've been blindsided in the backfield, been hit in the open field, or sandwiched between two massive defensemen—those hits were nothing compared to the pain I feel right now.

I can't take it any longer. As soon as I can half-straighten up, I walk/crawl/hobble out the swinging door. In the dining room, I pick up as much speed as I can to get away from Ruthie's cries of anguish. Back upstairs, I get to my room, grab a towel, and get into the shower to wash off not only my vomit, but all thought and memory of what I just witnessed.

The long shower helps, but hardly erases the memory.

---

I make Steve wear his uniform. It might help.

"In every war there are casualties, Tony," Steve tells me in the car. "He died for a just cause."

"It's a lot different when you know the guy," I tell him.

"Jerry was a fat, lump of worthless flesh who barely got out of high school, hardly one of your best friends, Tony."

"He's Ruthie's kid, Steve."

"The problem is he should have never been where he was. When Ruthie told me he was in the infantry, I couldn't believe it," Steve explains. "Jerry should have been peeling potatoes or delivering the mail or something. You can't give a guy that dumb, a gun."

"He's Ruthie's kid, Steve."

"And I feel just as bad about him as you, but that's all a part of fighting for what you believe in."

"I'm not sure what I believe in."

"You're not listening to that black tutor idiot, are you?"

"He's not an idiot."

"He's a black, peace-freak, communist-sympathizing bastard."

I feel numb inside.

Steve keeps talking. "Well, at least we don't have to worry about Jerry trying to pledge the fraternity when he got out and back into school. It would be tough black-ballin' our cook's kid."

We drive in silence another mile or two and get off the Interstate in one of the small towns thirty miles south of the university. Log trucks, loaded and unloaded, drive right through the middle of town. Their diesel smell is sickening. There is a market, three taverns, two gas stations, a state liquor store, and a hardware store on Main Street. The pavement is potholed, and the one traffic signal hangs on a wire stretched across the road. It bounces up and down every time a truck drives underneath it. There are a hundred towns like this in the state; all depressing. The directions tell us to stay on Main until we hit the grammar school, and veer to the left.

When I see the black smoke a mile or so away, I point and tell Steve, "That's it, over there."

Steve drives the Dart into the parking lot. There is a big sign with an American Flag with a caption reading: *America, Love it or Leave it* on the wall of the building. We get out of the car and walk inside. At first glance I can't really tell what they do in this place. It is a big open building with a cement floor. There are a number of old rusted truck beds, back-hoes, and hunks of machinery in different spots. Workers use blow torches to dismantle the junk and cut the metal into small pieces. The cut pieces are lifted onto a conveyor belt that takes them across the factory floor to a huge furnace—which is what was belching out the black smoke we saw on our way here. My chest starts to hurt from breathing the thick air.

"So, you're Touchdown Tony," he says approaching me with his hand out to shake.

"Yeah."

General August T. Brown is five-nine, maybe a hundred-eighty. He's bald, got a beer gut, maybe fifty, maybe sixty; it's hard to tell when a guy's really out of shape.

Steve goes into attention and salutes him. "Steve Carlton, sir, ROTC."

"At ease, Carlton," Brown orders Steve. "I've seen your cadets. You got a lot of work to do."

"Yes, sir."

"Nice of you boys to drop by."

I'm looking around the place. "What do you do here?" I ask.

"We take all the crap nobody wants anymore, cut it up, re-smelt it, and make rebar out of it," he tells me proudly.

I have no idea what rebar is.

"I'll show you."

General Brown walks next to me with Steve behind us, as we tour the factory. "Diamond Jim said you wanted to talk to me."

"I need to get into the National Guard."

"Why?"

"Somebody screwed up, I lost my deferment, and now they want me to take a physical."

"If you get called up," Brown says. "It's your duty to report."

"I know that," I tell him.

"But he can't," Steve adds.

"Why not?"

"Football," Steve says.

Brown stops. "I remember when I got called up, I wanted to go. I couldn't wait to go, get a gun in my hand, and start blasting japs and krauts."

"But you probably didn't have a Rose Bowl to go to," I tell

him.

"They had a Rose Bowl," Brown corrects me.

"I just mean it was different back then," I try to explain.

"No, it wasn't."

This is not going well.

"I'm not sure if football is an acceptable reason for not reporting for active duty, Tony," he says.

It's getting harder and harder to breath, the closer we get to the smelting machine. "I've worked my whole life to play football, General Brown."

"You're twenty-years old. Two years in the service isn't going to kill you."

"It could." As soon as I say this, I regret it.

"And that's a sacrifice men have made for their country since our country began."

Steve realizes I'm in trouble and says, "It's not that he doesn't want to serve, he just wants to do it in the National Guard."

"How are you going to do weekends in the Guard, if you're playing football on Saturdays?"

"I don't know," I tell him. "All I know is I got to get in and get in now."

Brown gives me a snide little smile, as if he is thoroughly enjoying this conversation. "Tony, do you think I thought about football when I was on Iwo?"

I want to ask "Where's Iwo," but I don't. "Probably not," I answer.

"All I thought about was doing my job, so other men could do theirs."

I don't answer. I'm not sure I know what he's talking about.

"You know what my job is now, Tony?"

I'm not sure if it's the rebar thing or the Guard thing, so I don't answer again.

"My job is to find men who have what it takes, the right attitude, and a whole lot of courage to fill the few spots available in this region's National Guard. Do you have that kind of courage?

94

Or can you get that kind of courage, Tony?"

I finally have, what I think, is a good answer for him, "Courage, I'm behind an offensive line half the size of...."

He cuts me off, "Not that kind of courage."

"What other kind of courage is there?" I ask.

"Figure it out, college boy."

## CHAPTER 14

I get through practice on autopilot. I'm sure Praytel was screaming bloody murder the whole time, but I wasn't listening, couldn't hear, or couldn't care less, maybe a combination of all three. My head is filled with so much stuff it's hard taking off my helmet.

"You okay, Tony?" Arthur asks me as I sit on the locker bench removing my pads.

"Fine."

"You seem troubled."

"I'm not."

"Worried about the game?"

"No."

"Want to talk about it?"

"Arthur, I don't need this crap right now. Just drop it, okay?"

Arthur takes a step back. "I'll pray for you, Tony."

"Yeah, you do that."

---

Steve picks me up after practice.

"I need a beer," I say, once I'm seated in the Dodge Dart.

"What?"

"I need a beer."

He drives in the direction of the house. "Not the house," I tell him.

"They're tapping a keg before the bonfire."

"I said, 'not the house,' Steve. I want to go someplace where people won't know me."

"Kinda hard to do in this town," Steve says.

We end up in a skuzzy tavern next to a motel that costs six bucks a night. We sit at the table in the back. Country music plays on the jukebox. The only other people in the bar are bleary-eyed, old drunks. Pitchers are sixty-five cents. The beer tastes funny, but at least it's cold. We split the first pitcher. I drink the next one by myself.

"This shit isn't supposed to happen to guys like me," I tell Steve.

"It's only twenty-three months. You could be in the NFL before you're twenty-three."

"If I don't get killed first."

"You're not going to get killed, Tony."

"Tell that to Ruthie's kid."

I signal the bartender for another pitcher.

"It's the right thing to do as an American."

"No, Steve, the right thing for me to do is call plays as an NFL quarterback. That's all I've ever wanted to do. It's what I was born to do. It's what I've been coached to do my whole life."

The bartender delivers the pitcher. "You Touchdown Tony?"

"No," I tell the cretin.

He walks back to the bar and tells a drunk, "He says it's not him, but it's him. I saw him on TV beating up a hippie."

I down another beer. I'm getting tipsy. "You have any idea what that 'courage' was the General was talking about?" I ask Steve.

"He was talking about what you need if you're going to be a soldier."

"He's not a soldier. He's National Guard."

"They're the same, Tony."

Another beer slides down my throat. "He might have been asking for money."

"I don't think so," Steve says.

"That 'courage' bullshit was telling me if I wanted in, I'd have to pay."

"Not a chance," Steve says. "The guy is Army all the way. He's not going to put his reputation on the line asking for money."

"Why not?" I ask.

"Because Generals don't do that."

97

"I'd do it if I were him."

I polish off another pitcher.

"There has got to be a way to get out of this."

"I don't think so, Tony."

"Me going into the Army is stupid. Nobody wants to see me go. People are making tons of money off me. The people who watch me play are going to be pissed. The University shouldn't let it happen after all I've done for them. We wouldn't have a shot at the Rose Bowl if it wasn't for me."

"Tell Schwartz, maybe he'll help you out."

I've drunk way too much, way too fast. I feel bloated. I couldn't run a 4.4 forty right now if my life depended on it. I got to take a leak.

"You still want to go to the bonfire?" Steve asks as I stumble from the table.

"I got to go. I don't have a choice."

---

Steve has to park six blocks away. We have to walk with the rest of the rabble. I put my hood up so no one can see it's me tripping on the cracks in the cracked sidewalk. Fans are streaming into the park. There must be thousands.

It's cold, rainy, and miserable. It looks like the entire university is jammed into the open area between thickly wooded tracts of land. There must be at least ten cords of wood piled up in the middle of the field. Some guy pours gasoline on the logs. The Swallow Lumber flatbed is the stage. The cheerleaders are dancing on it. They must be freezing their tight little asses off in this weather. My teammates are behind the truck, waiting to be introduced. Praytel and the assistant coaches are here, standing around to make sure nobody gets drunk. Praytel won't see me drinking because I'm already hammered. The band is playing the awful fight song. Six cop cars are lined up on the outside of the field like horses at a racetrack. I see the university president with some guy in a fancy uniform, probably the chief of police. They're hanging around with regular cops drinking cups of something steaming. President Schwartz looks pissed. I can't imagine what about. He should be thrilled. It's the best year the Pioneers have had since my dad was playing. Thanks to me. I consider going over and talking to him, but maybe it's best if I wait until later.

Although it's tough to focus, I see Marcus, Katie, and the two outside agitators from parts unknown way in the back of the crowd over by the park's picnic tables. They have a bunch of people, at least a couple hundred, around them, including the guy I threw off the stage after the Northern game; he's limping. Marcus has a guitar strapped to his back.

I can't find the brothers, but I'm sure they're here in the crowd, drunk as skunks.

A torch is thrown onto the gasoline soaked woodpile and a bonfire bursts fifty feet skyward. It hurts my eyes to watch. The rain in the air sizzles as it hits the flames. Already primed for madness with plenty of alcohol, the heat whips the crowd into a frenzy. When the dumb band finally comes to the end of the Pioneer fight song, the crowd kicks in with their own version.

"Old State U our pants are down to you, Woodchucks, bastards, sons-of-bitches too. You drive your farm machines, we'll screw your beauty queens, Woodchuck U, fuck you."

Old State U, our pants are down to you,
Woodchucks, bastards, sons-of-bitches too.
You drive your farm machines,
We'll screw your beauty queens,
Woodchuck U, fuck you.

One of the male cheerleaders, who's probably queer, takes a microphone and screams at the crowd. "What are we gonna do to them Woodchucks?"

"Skin 'em. Slay 'em. Suck 'em up and spit 'em out." The crowd wails.

The girls on the truck go into one of their choreographed routines. The crowd follows suit dancing their own bad version.

"What are we gonna do to those Woodchucks?" The same yell leader yells into the microphone, eliciting the same Skin/Slay/Suck response from the crowd, which then breaks into their Woodchuck U chant.

I see the team start to climb aboard the truck and make my way over. My head is spinning, the beer really starting to take effect. I haven't been drunk since the start of the season, and I'm really out of practice. A couple of the guys see me and say something, but it's too loud to hear, or my ears are working about as well as my feet. I'm at the back corner of the truck, one of the last in the line, when I hear a different kind of noise from the crowd.

I peer through the smoke and the rain and see Marcus standing on a picnic table, surrounded by his buddies. Marcus is strumming his guitar, singing, "How many roads must a man walk down..." His followers join him in the song, but the football crowd drowns them out with: "Shut the fuck up," "Go back to Russia," and "Commie lovers." There are a lot more invectives tossed at him, but I can't understand all of them. The words seem to fall into a big pile of sloppy mush inside my head.

The band breaks into the Pioneer fight song, "Pioneers lead us forward onto the battlefield..."

Marcus' group gets louder, but stays calm, amidst the verbal venom coming their way. The chanting football fans turn and face the singing demonstrators. Birds are flipped. People spit. This is getting real mean, real quick.

Hayden jumps up on the picnic table, pushes Marcus aside, and yells to his group, "I got a better song."

The demonstrators cheer. Hayden sings, "Come on all of you big strong men, Uncle Sam needs a helping hand..." The demonstrators join in. "He got himself in a terrible jam..."

The football fans turn up their volume, "May the actions of our warriors, emulate your spirit here..."

"...Way down yonder in Vietnam." Louder.

"...with their courage and ideals," Much louder.

100

"Put down your books, grab a gun."

On the truck bed the guy in the fancy uniform grabs the microphone. "This is Police Chief Philip Hurlbutt. You are currently staging an unlawful assembly…"

"We're gonna have a whole lot of fun…"

"Onto the field of victory…"

"And it's one, two, three…"

Singing, screaming, shouting, swearing. It's a madhouse. The heat from the bonfire upping the temperature and temperament of the entire crowd.

"What are we fighting for?"

"You are hereby ordered to disperse," the chief continues, only further inciting both sides of the quarrel. "Leave this park now."

"…March the fighting Pioneers."

A bottle flies through the air and shatters at Hayden's feet. I see him jump from the table and go to Katie, who hands him a handful of something. Marcus climbs back up, starts to strum his guitar, but is pelted by clods of dirt, rocks, and bottles. "How many roads…"

The music dies.

"Disperse this instant!" Hurlbutt screams into the microphone, but only makes matters worse. The fans surge towards the demonstrators. The cops spread out. I pull my hood tight over my head and come out from the safety of my teammates. I stumble towards the coming confrontation. I have no idea what possesses me to do this. Marcus is knocked off the stage by flying objects. The Molly girl helps pick Marcus up off the ground. I can feel the anger, fear, and negative energy pulsating around me. It's frightening. Projectiles fly every-which-way.

And the bonfire explodes.

It sounds like shots and looks like small explosions. Bam, bam, bam. Firebombs detonate inside the bonfire sending debris and ear-shattering shocks into the crowd. Everyone must think its gunfire. Fans hit the deck, scatter in all directions, or stampede away from the bonfire and toward the demonstrators. People are getting trampled. I try to go left, but can't. I'm pushed whatever way the crowd is pushing. I see Hayden behind an overturned picnic table throwing handfuls of round little objects into the bonfire blaze. He's laughing hysterically.

Sirens from all six cop cars blare. The noise is deafening.

The band skedaddles. Some drop their instruments in the mud. The cheerleaders jump from the stage. The team members on the flatbed aren't sure what to do. A couple linemen, including Lester, jump down off the stage, and join the surge toward the demonstrators. Praytel and his coaches try to corral the team members together, but it's a losing battle. The shots, gunfire, whatever it is, keep going off. Each explosion adds more terror, fear, and madness to the chaos.

The protestors run. And I can't blame them a bit.

The football fans reach Marcus' group. The peace freaks don't have a chance. The cops are in the middle of the fray pushing the demonstrators into the woods. The explosions finally stop, but it makes little difference. I'm hit in the back by a rock, bottle, piece of wood, something; it doesn't matter what. It hurts. I go down, flat on my face into the mud. I'm dazed; the only thing that keeps me awake are feet stomping upon me. Seconds later I feel two hands on my jacket pull me upward. I can't see who it is. The hands pull and I have no choice but to follow. A female voice is telling me what to do. I can barely hear her with the wailing sirens, fire crackling, and screams from the crowd. The demonstrators disappear into the thick tree line. You can hear some fall, scream in pain, but mostly I hear the sounds of a retreat.

I throw up. The liquid inside me purges out of my mouth with a foamy head on it. My diaphragm jerks upward inside me like an elevator making stop after stop, but I keep moving. I have no choice. A hand is pulling me along like a little red wagon. And I run straight into a tree trunk. I go down hard, this time landing in a thicket of wet leaves and twigs. I'm on my side, doubled up in pain. I can't see. I'm soaked, freezing cold, and caked with mud. I feel a cloth go against my face, wiping the dirt from my eyes.

A minute or two later, I hear her voice.

"Let me guess, you're just here to meet girls?"

It's Molly.

---

I wake up dizzy, cotton-mouthed, head pounding, with mud in my ears. I stink of dirt, sweat, and vomit. My wet jacket, t-shirt, jeans, boots, and socks lie in a pile to the right of me. I'm naked underneath the covers. I don't know where I am.

There is a sharp pain in the middle of my back. The lights are off. I'm alone.

My eyes focus. Light from the street light shines inside. I look around. I'm in my room. I don't know how I got here.

I get up slowly, find the light switch, grab a towel off the hook in the small, built-in closet, leave the room, and walk up the hallway. In the bathroom, I must piss for at least an hour. It feels wonderful. I shower. The hot water is magic. I dry myself off, wrap the towel around me, and walk slowly back to my room. I ache all over, but feel human again.

Two steps into my room, I stop. I can't believe what I see.

"Is this a creepy outfit or what?" Molly sits on the chair wearing Steve's ROTC uniform.

"What are you doing here?" I ask, and become a bit self-conscious standing with a towel wrapped around me.

She reads my unease. "Don't worry. I was the one who took your pants off." Molly then adds, "I've seen better."

I back into the closet, find a pair of clean jeans and pull them on, then a t-shirt and a sweatshirt. "What are you doing here?" I repeat.

"Hanging around bored, mostly. You've been asleep for hours. I was wandering the floor looking for something interesting. I found this uniform."

I come back out into the room. She is in the chair. I sit on the bed and put on a pair of socks to warm my feet. "You're wearing my friend's uniform."

"What does he want, to be General MacArthur?"

"Yeah, guess so."

"What do you want to be?" she asks.

"The next Joe Namath," I tell her.

"I met a girl in New York who said she had sex with him."

"Is that where you're from?"

"I've been in so many places, I don't even know where I'm from anymore," she tells me.

I sit on the bed across from her. She's about nine sizes too small for the uniform, but she looks cute in a strange way. "What did the girl say about him?"

"Who?"

"Joe Namath."

"Said he was kind of a jerk."

"You were the one who picked me up out of the mud tonight?"

"You remember, how touching."

"Why'd you do that?" I ask.

"Let's just say you seemed to be in need of a hand."

"Thanks."

"You're welcome."

Molly picks up one trophy after another, and reads the inscriptions silently. "These all yours?"

"Yeah."

"You got them here from grammar school to now." She puts the last trophy down and starts in on the photos I have up. She moves from one to the next, spending a few seconds on each. "You know, there is not one picture up here without you in it."

"What?"

"Every picture is a picture of you. Don't you have any with other people, just by themselves?"

"I guess not."

"Why not?"

"I don't know. I never realized that."

She takes Steve's hat off. "Your whole life is already decided and done, isn't it? You know what you're going to be doing for the next twenty years."

"Yeah, play football."

She faces me and gives me a short laugh. "I don't know where I'm sleeping one night to the next."

"Is that why you came here?" I ask.

"No."

"Is that what you want?" I ask. "Everybody wants something out of me."

"I want to be normal," she says. "Can you help me out in that area?"

"I don't think I know how."

"Neither do I."

For the next few minutes Molly filled me in on what happened at the bonfire. Some sounded familiar; most sounded frightening. "I've been in my share of college riots and this one was about a four on a scale of ten."

"What happened to Marcus?"

"He's okay. He made it into the woods."

"That boyfriend of yours was having a good time."

"Explosive personality," she explains.

Molly takes off Steve's uniform. She has no problem with being shy. "What are you so mad about?" she asks as she puts her clothes back on.

"Who said I was mad?"

"Anyone who talks that way in their sleep is mad at something."

I lie back on the bed, fold my arms across my chest. "I got drafted."

"Into the Army?"

I look away in embarrassment.

"Aren't you the football god around here?"

"I forgot to take some bullshit final last term," I admit.

"Not a smart move for a college boy."

"Stupid, unbelievably stupid," I admit.

"Oh, I don't know. Guys get drafted every day."

"Not future NFL quarterbacks."

I turn slightly to face her. "Now, I can't get out of it. I tried to get the teacher to change my grade and she wouldn't do it. The National Guard guy is being a dick. My coach won't help because I'm blowing this place off. I don't know what to do."

She stares at me as if she knows what I'm thinking.

"I can't believe I'm so stupid."

She gets up. "Come on, we'll go see Hayden. If there's a scam out there, he'll know it."

---

The SDS offices at the student union are a war zone. Protestors, returned from the bonfire, are spread out nursing their cuts and bruises. Everyone is wet, dirty, depressed, and muddy. This is the loser's locker room after a thorough trashing.

Two scruffy, ill-kempt and ill-mannered Vietnam vets sit sharing a joint. "I really miss that righteous 'Nam weed," one says to the other.

"Let's not be bogarting that joint," the other vet demands.

Molly leads our way. We have to step over a number of people stretched out on the floor.

"What are you doing here?" Marcus asks me. He's in the middle of the room, cleaning out a gash in the head of a fellow demonstrator. The kid winces in pain as the alcohol touches his skin.

"I'm not sure," I answer truthfully.

"Hayden around?" Molly asks Marcus.

Marcus shrugs his shoulders.

Molly continues. I follow. We reach a door in the back of the big room. She doesn't knock. She opens and enters. Hayden sits

106

on the old dilapidated couch, wearing his sunglasses, and smoking a joint. His naked body is barely covered by an old blanket. Katie snuggles next to him, asleep, trying to keep her naked body warm.

"Nice to see you, Hayden," Molly greets him.

He looks at her through his dark glasses. "Don't worry about her, she's just pussy."

"Remember Tony?" she asks.

"Football star."

"He needs to get out of the draft," Molly explains for me.

"Uncle Sam wants you?"

"Yeah."

"That's a bitch," Hayden says.

"You must know some scam, Hayden," Molly continues.

"I don't know," Hayden says. "Selective Service pigs are really cracking down." He takes another hit from the joint. "You had your physical yet?" He asks me.

"Ten days from now."

"Anything the matter with you?"

"No."

Commit any felonies?"

"No."

"You a fag?"

"No."

Hayden stops asking questions.

"There's got to be something, Hayden," Molly says.

"You could have someone climb up on a ladder and jump on your knee. Knees are about the only body part they let you out with now."

"I can't do that," I tell him. "I'm going into the NFL."

"They got an NFL in Canada?" Hayden asks me.

"No. They play a different kind of football up there."

"You got asthma?"

"No."

Psoriasis?"

"What's that?"

"Some shit you get on your skin."

"No."

"Then, I'd say you're fucked." Hayden burns the tips of his fingers inhaling the last nub of the joint. His sudden jump in pain awakens Katie.

"Hey, Tony."

I try not to acknowledge her presence, but it's hard not to. "Nice to see you."

Molly pulls at my sleeve. "Let's go." She holds on as we turn to exit the room, but before we leave, she says to Hayden. "Don't worry, he's just dick."

We hurry out of the SDS office. I can't wait to split. Molly doesn't let go of me until we are outside on the street. "Now where?" I ask her.

"Your place, I'm tired."

---

"I've never had sex with a big time football star before, and I've been at it since I was fourteen."

"Fourteen?"

"Step-daddy."

Molly gets naked like a guy in a locker room. She has no hesitation, reluctance, or avoidance. She puts it all right out there, as if saying "this is me."

She climbs into my narrow bed next to me, cuddles into the crook of my arm.

"Are you just here because you want to get back at your boyfriend?" I ask.

"Maybe," she answers.

"I don't get you."

"What's not to get?"

"You're going to screw me for the sake of screwing me?"

"That's what you usually do, isn't it?"

"No."

"Bullshit, Tony."

"It's different for a guy."

"No, it's not," she says quite calmly.

I'm about to answer, but she doesn't give me a chance.

"We're a lot alike, Tony."

"We are?"

"Right now, we're two lost souls wandering around earth, wondering what is going to happen to us next."

I can't admit it verbally, but she's right. "Are you scared?"

"I've been scared since the day my dad died," she tells me.

"How old were you?"

"Ten."

"I'm sorry."

"Me, too."

Usually, at this time with a woman, I'm banging away. Now, I lie perfectly still. "What do you want to do?"

She hesitates for a moment. "I want to believe in someone."

Not the answer I was expecting.

"And vice-versa," she adds.

For the first time in my life, I'm with a woman, and not sure what to do, or say next. Neither of us moves. We lie together sharing each other's warmth. "Are you sure you want to have sex?

"Sure," she says. "It's not every day I get to screw someone more screwed up than me."

I shift, roll on top of her, kiss her once gently, and mount her like I would any other chick. I do like I always do.

She pulls away. "What are you doing?"

"Having sex with you."

"Whoever taught you how to fuck?"

No woman has ever asked me this question before, and I don't take it well. "You want to tell me what to do?" I snap back at her.

"Try making love and not war."

I'm back on my back. "Go ahead, Molly, tell stupid what to do. Why should you be any different than anyone else?"

"Anybody who can learn, Tony, isn't stupid." She reaches up and holds my face in her hand. She kisses me more gently than I've ever been kissed.

She was warm, inviting, sensual, and kind. She gave and accepted pleasure in equal amounts. There was no rush, conquest, proving masculinity, or wanting her to leave the moment I was finished.

For the first time in my life, I make love to a woman.

## CHAPTER 15

Best night of sleep I've had since this mess started. My back hurts where I got hit, but I feel much better. We stay in my room until after nine. Most of the bros have finished with the bathroom, so I guard the door while Molly showers. Then I do the same. We go downstairs to the kitchen. I'm finally hungry. Six or seven of the bros are already eating when we enter, and each checks out who they consider to be my latest conquest. I don't bother making introductions. Molly cracks eggs on the stove's griddle, puts bread in the toaster, and pours juice.

The boys are staring at her, and I can't stop them.

"My apologies if I kept any of you up last night when I was screwing Tony's brains out," she says, as we sit down to eat alongside the brothers.

A couple of the bros almost swallow their eggs whole, hearing Molly's apology.

I look outside and see Ruthie's car pull into her spot. "Ruthie's here."

Seconds after I make the announcement, the six bros finish their breakfasts and hurry out of the room like they're running from the Black Plague.

"Was it something I said?" Molly asks me.

Ruthie enters. "Tony," she says.

Ruthie looks ten years older. A whitish/grey pallor of grief covers her entire face. It's horrifying.

"I'm sorry, Ruthie."

"They're bringing Jerry back this morning, Tony," she says. "They told me to meet him at the airport."

"Okay." I don't know what else to say.

"Would you go with me?"

I hesitate. "Me?"

"I can't go alone." Ruthie puts her hands on the table to steady herself. Her bloodshot eyes stare right into mine.

I don't know what to do. I don't know what to say. What can I do? I don't want to go. I have my own problems.

"We'll go with you."

I turn to face Molly, who moves to Ruthie's side, places her hand upon hers, and repeats. "We'll go with you."

My mouth drops open. I don't know what to do with my hands. My feet won't move. Why? Why are we doing this? How am I supposed to help make the cook feel better?

"You got a car?" Molly asks me.

"Yeah."

"Go get it."

I do as I'm told.

---

The airport is a twenty-minute drive east. Ruthie weeps in the back seat. I don't utter a word.

"How did he die?" Molly asks her.

"I don't know."

"What have they told you?"

"They haven't."

"They must have said something," Molly says.

"They said it was a closed casket."

"Have you made arrangements?"

"Their people here are making them for me."

Molly reaches into the back seat and holds Ruthie's hand.

We arrive at the airport. I park the car. The three of us walk into the small terminal building. I have no idea where to go. There is one woman behind a counter where a listing of the arrivals and departures are on a chalkboard.

"Tell her why we're here, Tony, and ask her where we should be."

Without hesitation, I walk over to the woman. "Excuse me..."

"Aren't you Touchdown Tony?"

Five minutes later we're standing on the airport tarmac

beneath a flimsy awning.

It's an ugly day, colder than usual. Wind's blowing from the west. The rain clouds hang low in the sky, pushing down a wet fog of dampness. It is the kind of cold, which permeates your entire body with a clammy, uncomfortable feeling. We stand shivering a good ten minutes.

I hear it first, then see the big, green airplane with Army stars on its wings, come in for a landing. As it taxies toward us, the wind from the propellers sprays the air's moisture, soaking us to the skin. Now, we are not only cold and miserable, but cold, wet, and miserable.

The plane parks no less than thirty feet from where we stand. The propellers stop spinning. A stairway ramp is rolled up to the passenger door of the plane. It opens. Two soldiers exit the plane and come down the ramp. One moves to the back of the aircraft, while the other approaches us.

"Ruth Babcock?"

"Yes."

"We have your son."

A black hearse drives onto the tarmac and parks not far from the plane. The driver of the funeral wagon pulls around so that the back of his car faces the side of the plane. This man, dressed in a black suit, gets out of the driver's seat, walks to the back of the hearse, and opens the rear door.

There is nothing for us to do. We stand and watch. Molly holds Ruthie's arm.

The cargo doors of the plane open. I can see a number of silver coffins lined up inside. We must be one stop of many. An odd looking vehicle arrives next. It has a long slanted metal ramp attached to its roof, with lines of small wheels running through its middle. The vehicle with the highest end of the slant towards the plane, pulls up to the edge of the cargo door, and stops. Two men inside the cargo area, lug one coffin to the edge, and line one end up to the slide conveyor. I can't hear, but the two seem to be arguing. Another soldier comes out of the plane, and positions

113

himself at the bottom of the metal slide. This guy I can hear. "Go ahead, I'm ready."

One soldier in the plane pushes the coffin onto the slide, while the other man holds a tethering rope attached to the back end of the coffin. As the casket begins its downward projection, the front guy says something to the back guy, who reacts with a shout of "Bullshit," and drops the rope in his hands. The coffin immediately picks up speed and rumbles down the ramp like a boulder down a hill. The soldier at the bottom has to jump out of the way before the silver torpedo kills him. The coffin slips off the metal slide's wheels and crashes into the ground. Thank God, it doesn't pop open.

"Nice move, dumb shits," the soldier on the ground yells at the guys in the plane.

Molly and I watch in awe of the idiocy. Ruthie's reaction is one of absolute horror. Her entire body convulses, she wails guttural sounds, and her hands become fists and push into her wet face.

It gets worse. There is a huge dent in the corner of the coffin. The three soldiers continue to blame each other, but can't seem to pick up the coffin. They drop it one more time. The funeral man in the black suit comes over to help. Two men per side, they lift the casket and carry it to the waiting hearse. They have more trouble sliding it into the bed of the wagon, because of the dent.

The soldiers bitch and bicker all the way back into the plane, where they re-board, and immediately shut the door behind them. The plane's propellers begin to spin.

"Are you Ruth Babcock?"

"Yes."

"I'm Funeral Director, Randolph Webb. I am very sorry about your loss."

Ruthie has calmed and returns to her weeping mode.

"What happens now?" Molly asks the man.

"Arrangements have been made locally, but she will have to come with me to sign some papers and agree to the schedule."

Ruthie nods her head, the best answer she's able to give.

"Do you know if she has a plot?" the director asks me.

"I do." Ruthie answers, saving me the trouble of admitting I don't know.

"Can you come with me?" Randolph asks.

Ruthie takes two steps in his direction.

"Do you want us to come with you?" Molly asks.

Ruthie shakes her head. "No."

I'm relieved.

"Thank you for coming," Ruthie says.

We wait until the two are seated in the front seat, and the hearse pulls off the tarmac. The Army plane is now on the runway ready for takeoff. The whir of the engines hurts my eardrums.

---

"Aren't you Touchdown Tony?" She asks after she puts down the newspaper she's reading.

The front page headline is: "Riot at University Bonfire." The page is filled with photos of the mass exodus.

"Is President Schwartz in?" I ask.

"He's in, but I'm not so sure this is the best time to be paying him a visit."

"I have to see him. It's important."

The older lady nods her head to the left. "He's in the last room on the right."

"Okay."

"And good luck on Saturday," the woman says. "We're counting on you to beat the spread."

The hallway is quite long. We pass office after office with titles stenciled on the doors. The nearer we get, the louder we hear voices at the far end.

"I don't think they're rehearsing for a play," Molly says as we get close.

The door is open. We walk in. The room is quite large. There is a conference table pushed to the back of the room with five chairs on one side. No one is seated in the chairs. In the center of the room, and all the way to the back where we came in, are folding chairs, and each of these is occupied. Some spectators are forced to stand. Portable lights have been set up and are shining on the three old men standing behind the table: President Schwartz, Police Chief Hurlbutt, and the town's mayor, Seymour Denton. The TV cameras record the scene. Molly and I stay in the back behind the members of the press, school officials, lots of cops, and a few SDS members, including Hayden, who is the only one in the room wearing sunglasses.

Marcus stands alone in front of the table. "We have a right to be heard," he tells the trio.

"No, you don't," the mayor corrects Marcus. "You tell your Commie, outside-agitating, rabble-rousers, they're not welcome in our town."

"The Constitution of the United States gives us the right to free speech," Marcus corrects him.

"Not this weekend, it doesn't."

"We have a legal permit to march."

"It's been cancelled," Hurlbutt says.

"You can't do that. We have a right to free assembly."

"Not anymore," the mayor says.

"You can't just turn this off like a light switch," Marcus shoots back.

"Listen boy, I want you and your criminals out of this town," Hurlbutt tells Marcus.

"It wasn't us who started the fight," Marcus retaliates. "You're the one who let your goons loose."

"There will be no march in my city this Saturday, and that's final," Mayor Denton speaks.

"Then we will keep it on university property where you don't have the same authority," Marcus argues.

"I'll call out the National Guard," Hurlbutt announces. The press takes particular notice to the comment.

"I will not have armed troops on my campus," President Schwartz finally speaks up.

"You will if you don't want another Columbia on your hands," Hurlbutt informs Schwartz.

"I don't want to see anyone get hurt," Schwartz says." "This is an institution of learning, not violence."

"I will issue an order. If anyone is seen protesting within the confines of city patrolled area, they will be arrested and punished to the full extent of the law." Mayor Denton says and points his index finger at Marcus.

"You can't do that," Marcus says waving a piece of paper. "I have a signed city permit authorizing our right to a free assembly."

"Cancelled," Hurlbutt says and slams his fist onto the table. "This meeting is over."

"You can't do that," Marcus pleads.

Hurlbutt and Denton come around the table, and approach Marcus from both sides. "Don't test me," the policeman warns.

"I'm telling you," Marcus says. "It's way too late to be calling off the march."

Denton adds, "You hear him, boy? Don't test us. You will lose."

The room clears out quickly. I wait in the back. No one notices me. News reporters must be a lot different than sports reporters. Molly meets Marcus and Hayden on their way out the door.

Hayden is ecstatic. "That riot was the best thing that coulda happened. We'll have people here from as far away as San Francisco. This is going to be great."

Marcus' head hangs low as he leaves the room. A couple of reporters ask him questions, but he refuses to answer. He sees me, but doesn't acknowledge my presence.

President Schwartz is surrounded by people on his way out the door, and I can't get to him. I go up the hallway behind the group and wait for Schwartz to enter his inner office.

"Back so soon?" his secretary asks.

"I have to talk to him."

"I'm telling you, I'm not so sure he's in the mood to chat."

I enter his office. It's nice, but doesn't compare to Eugene Swallow's office. "Excuse me, President Schwartz."

His back is to me, and when he hears my voice, he slowly turns to face me. He looks horribly tired.

"I'm Tony McIntyre."

"Who?"

"Tony McIntyre." I pause. "Touchdown Tony McIntyre."

"What do you want?"

"I need to talk to you."

"This is not a good time."

"Well, I don't have a lot of time."

I come to his desk and sit down.

"What are you doing?" he asks.

"I want to make a deal. I need a little help with my transcript, and I'm sure you want the Pioneers to keep selling out football games."

Schwartz gazes at me with a look on his face as if he doesn't understand what I'm saying. How could he not?

"I forgot to take my philosophy final last term, didn't get enough credits, the draft board found out about it, and now they want me to take a physical in ten days."

His gaze gets even weirder.

"If we don't get to the Rose Bowl this year, I know I can get the Pioneers there next year, and that has got to mean big money for the school." I'm talking a mile a minute. "My agent tells me if I declare this year, I'll go in the first round, and can sign with an NFL team for maybe the biggest bonus ever. But this draft board thing has really got everything all screwed up. So, we need to make a deal."

"You're talking about football?" he asks.

"Yes." I continue. "I agree to stay and play out my senior year. I stay at quarterback, and in exchange, you change the incomplete on my transcript to a D."

118

I'm out of breath.

Schwartz peers down at me like I'm some disease.

"Deal?"

He steps to his left, but doesn't take his eyes off me. "Do you know what is going on, on this campus, son?"

"Yes."

"We're sitting on a powder keg. This place could explode any minute."

"If we win Saturday, it probably will."

"Five thousand people are expected to be here."

"There'll be forty thousand in the stands, and every home game next year will be the same, if I stick around and play."

"I can't believe I'm hearing what I'm hearing," he says. "They want to bring armed troops on campus and you're asking me to think about football?"

"Yes, this is a great deal for everybody."

"Get out," he orders.

"Do we have a deal or not? All you have to do is change one letter on my transcript."

He's coming around the desk towards me. "Get out of my office."

I stand up. "President Schwartz, I'll even guarantee the Pioneers will make it to the Rose Bowl."

"Leave."

He takes my arm and pushes me to the door.

"Please," I beg. "I can't go in the Army. I have a career in the NFL waiting for me."

At the door he removes his hand from my arm, he says to me, "When it comes to education, Mr. McIntyre, we have certainly failed you." He gives me a slight push through the doorway.

The office door slams shut behind me. I walk past the secretary. "I told you this was a bad time," she tells me.

I don't answer. I keep walking.

"Don't forget, you got to cover that spread this Saturday," she says to me before I reach the hallway.

I'm in shock. It makes no sense. If I get drafted by the NFL, I'm not here. If I get drafted by the Army, I'm not here either. The university loses both ways. I can't believe he didn't go for my deal.

Outside the rain and cold doesn't shake me out of my funk. Some girl comes up and asks for my autograph, but I ignore her. I have this incredible rush of worry coming down on me like two unblocked linebackers on a blitz. My body tightens. I lean forward against a street light pole. I close my eyes. I can't tell you how long I stay in this position. I have never felt so alone.

I have to sort this out, talk to somebody, and figure out a next move, if there is one.

## CHAPTER 16

The SDS office is mobbed. Wall-to-wall people. Few look like students. Besides the two Vietnam Vets I saw the other evening, there must be twenty more. They're all scruffy, dirty, and stoned. Lots of people are wearing *Out of Vietnam, NOW* t-shirts. Molly's business must be booming. There are fliers coming off the mimeograph machine describing Saturday's march. There is a huge map of the campus on one wall with arrows outlining the path of the march that will start at Main, go through the business district, come on the campus at 13ᵗʰ, proceed through the center of campus, and ending where University meets the student union where the rally will be held.

I wander around looking for Molly. I can't find her in the crowd. Nobody notices me. These people must not read Sports Illustrated.

An air horn blasts, which freezes everyone in their tracks.

"Listen up, everybody."

Marcus comes out of the back office. He climbs up on a table in the center of the room. "Can everybody hear me?" he asks.

All talking and activity quiets.

"I just came back from a meeting at President Schwartz' office," he pauses. "Our march has been cancelled."

The crowd gasps and every negative word in the English language is heard, the most popular being, "Bullshit."

"The mayor is threatening to call in the National Guard. The police say they will arrest anyone on the streets protesting. If you think the cops were over-zealous the night of the bonfire, trust me, they'll be vicious on Saturday."

The crowd is mumbling their disappointment. One person speaks up, "I thought we had a permit from the city?"

"We did."

"Then why the hell can't we march?"

"They rescinded it."

"The city can't do that."

"They already have."

The grumbling continues. "We have a right to be heard," "They can't do this," "We're Americans too," is voiced from the assembled.

"We can't," Marcus answers. "We can't march against the violence in Southeast Asia, and cause more violence here. It doesn't make any sense. The best thing we can do is plan another march, on another day, somewhere we can be heard, and not be beaten silly by a bunch of Nazi Storm Troopers."

The assembled begin to accept their fate.

"I'm sorry," Marcus says.

"Fuck them!" Hayden wails from the other side of the room. "I say fuck them." He's carrying a baseball bat, climbing up next to the *Force of Peace* statue. "I say getting the crap beat out of us the other night was the best thing that could have happened. We're all still here, aren't we?"

The crowd non-verbally agrees.

"The reason they don't want us to march is because they know we can make a difference, that we will be heard, on TV, on the radio, in the newspapers; and not just here, but across the country, all the way to Washington."

The crowd is starting to stir.

Hayden picks up the tempo. "They're scared of what we believe, and how strongly we believe it. They're scared of what we say, what we do, and how we're doing it." Hey," he says, "we're not breaking any laws. We have a permit. We have our right to free speech, the right to assemble, the right to tell these assholes to end the war, and end the war now."

The assembled cheer.

"If we march, students will be expelled," Marcus yells over to Hayden.

"Good."

"And arrested."

"All the better."

Hayden cuts Marcus' next comment off. "They don't scare us. We scare them. I say we get on the phones, call everyone we know, every college campus near and far, and every protest group, no matter how small, tell them to get their asses here on Saturday, and join in the most righteous protest this state has ever seen."

The assembled cheer.

"Are we going to let the pigs tell us what we can do?" Hayden screams out.

"No!"

"Are we going to let them silence us?"

"No!"

"Are we going to let them put us down?"

"No!"

"Are we going to be out there on Saturday and kick some ass?"

"Yes!"

Hayden has the crowd in an uproar, and to drive his point home even further, he winds up, swings his baseball bat, and strikes the *Force of Peace* statue, smashing it into a million bits. "Are you with me?"

"Yes."

This is frightening. I'm in the middle of a ready-to-boil-over mob scene. These people are more keyed up to get out there and destroy than the Pioneers during the pre-game, *fire 'em up* speech. People slap one another in their excitement. They scream, they howl, they chant: "March, march, march." Hayden has them so jacked up I wouldn't be surprised if they started beating on each other.

Marcus hurries over to Hayden. I can't hear him, but I can tell he's pleading to stop this madness. Hayden laughs in his face, thrilled at his own power of persuasion.

I have to get out of here. This is much too much for me to handle right now. But I don't know where to go. I don't know what to do. President Schwartz was my last chance. I've run out of options. I have to think, come up with another play that will work. I can't wait; the clock is ticking down.

I rush out of the SDS office. Outside, I pull my hood up and bury my identity. For the next two hours I wander around campus. There are posters up all over. Two kinds. One set has pictures of me throwing a pass, on Lester's shoulders, or with arms raised in victory; these mention the Rose Bowl, the Heisman, or make a disgusting comment about the Woodchucks. The other set of posters advertises Saturday's peace march, some plead *Give Peace a Chance,* and some state *Hell No We Won't Go.* These are glued, slapped, or taped on every available wall, light pole, and bulletin board. They well outnumber the football posters. It is a war of words and images played out on a campus battlefield.

As I walk, I see anger in the faces of students. I feel an overhanging cloud of resentment and fear. People are not happy. They seem frustrated, ill at ease, and worried.

Although nobody could feel any worse than I do right now.

I don't wear a watch, so I have no idea what time in the afternoon it may be. All I know is the rain has picked up, and I'm sick of being wet. I return to the house. I go in the back way to avoid any brothers who may be hanging around the front room. As soon as I'm in my room, I shut the door behind me. I strip off my wet clothes, lie down naked on the bed, and cover myself with sheet and blankets. I can't get warm.

The clock reads 2:30. Practice starts in a half hour. Screw practice. Next to the clock is the book Marcus left for me. I rise, grab *Vietnam, America's Nightmare,* open to the first page, and read.

I never knew the war in Vietnam started in the 1950's. The French were the ones fighting it, but they realized it was totally bogus, and got the hell out after a battle at Dien Bien Phu, where they got their asses kicked. President Kennedy started sending advisors in to help the Vietnamese government fight the war. Why he did this makes no sense to me. Kennedy was the guy who started the Peace Corps; I didn't think he was a warmonger. JFK gets assassinated and Lyndon Johnson adds all these new players, and makes it a real war. There are four-hundred-thousand American soldiers over there. Why? It makes no sense to me. We're in a war where there is nothing to win. We were never attacked like at Pearl Harbor, and there's no Vietcong Adolph Hitler we should kill. What is It all about? I keep reading, but I get no answers, and get more and more confused. All I know is I don't want to go over there and kill a bunch of people I don't know, don't understand, and have no reason to hate. Now I realize what Cassius Clay was talking about when he said, "I got nothing against no Vietcong."

I walk into the dining room, late for dinner. All conversation stops at the table. Everyone stares at me. "What the hell's the matter with you people?" I ask.

"Where have you been, Tony?" Steve asks me from his spot at the head of the table.

"In my room."

Everyone at the table has been served. I walk through the swinging kitchen door. A big, fat black woman is at the stove. "You Touchdown Tony?" she asks.

"Yeah, any dinner left?"

She fixes me a plate of what looks like stew over mashed potatoes. I take the food, return to the dining room, and sit at the end of the table.

"Announcements," Rick Snyder says banging the small gong in front of him.

Steve speaks up. "We got an offer from the America First Organization, a case of beer for every guy who marches with them this Saturday."

"They cancelled the march," Ernie pipes in.

"Don't worry, there's still going to be a march," Ralph says.

"Then we better get our beer in advance," Ernie concludes.

"What do you want me to tell them?" Steve asks.

"Tell them we'll march with them, but we want toilet paper instead of beer," Sean says.

Snyder asks, "Who's going to the wake tonight for Ruthie's kid?"

No one responds.

"I know no one is going to the funeral on Saturday, but one of us has got to go to the wake, tonight," he adds.

Quiet.

"There'll be free food and beer there," Rick ups the ante.

The brothers are dead silent.

"Don't make me force one of you to go," he threatens.

Silence.

A few more seconds transpire. "Come on, assholes, somebody volunteer."

"I'll go."

Every eye comes my way. I continue to eat the stew. It's way too spicy.

"You sure, Tony?" Steve asks.

"I said I'd go. I'll go."

I keep my eyes on my food, as every other eye in the room stays on me.

"Any other announcements?" Snyder asks.

Nope.

The gong bongs. Dinner is over. The brothers rush from the table. The two guys on kitchen duty clear the dishes, but have to wait for me to finish. Steve comes over and sits across from me. "You okay, Tony?"

"Fine?"

"Where were you this afternoon?"

"I told you, I was in my room," I snap back at him.

"Are you sure you're okay?"

"Yes, Goddamnit."

A few seconds elapse. I shovel in the last of my dinner. This meal wasn't as good as one of Ruthie's worst.

"You sure you want to go to that wake tonight?"

"I said I'd go, didn't I?" I pause. "Want to go with me?"

"I can't. Cindy has me going to a baroque concert."

"What's a baroque?"

"I don't know." Steve looks at me funny, like he wants to say something, but he's too afraid to say it. Instead, he tells me, "Diamond Jim's going to be there."

"I never got his damn tickets."

Steve takes a deep breath, builds up courage, and says, "Tony, I haven't said anything about you getting drafted to anyone."

He's lying. I can tell.

Steve speaks softly, "But it's all going to work out. I'm sure of it," he tries to assure me. "You're not going to have to go into the Army. I just know it," he says. "But you got to focus on the game, Tony. People are really counting on you. We win, we go to the Rose Bowl."

I don't need to hear this.

"And if we go to the Rose Bowl this year, people won't be so pissed off when you blow out of here and go pro next year."

What is he going to tell me next, "Cover the spread."?

"Tony, we got to win the game on Saturday. Is there anything I can do for you now?"

"Yeah," I tell him. "Shut the fuck up."

I push away from the table, and without looking back at him rush up the stairs to my room, closing the door behind me.

I only have one pair of dress slacks and one clean shirt with a collar. I don't bother with a tie. I hate wearing ties. I put on the coat I have with the hood, and get out of the house.

---

The wake is at the American Legion Hall. I arrive before seven. There are a number of cars and pick-up trucks in the lot trying to find a place to park. I drive by. I can't go in yet. I drive to the skuzzy bar Steve and I were in the other afternoon.

The same drunken old men are at the bar, although more of them than before. A couple loggers, still wearing their spiked boots, are playing pool. The same bartender tends bar.

"Gimme a pitcher," I call out to him.

He pours and delivers with a glass. "Let me guess," he says. "You're not Touchdown Tony."

I pull a dollar out of my pocket, and put it on the bar. "Keep the change."

To avoid him, I peer up at the TV set tuned to the news.

Hayden is on TV, a Zippo lighter in his hand. He flips his thumb, the flame ignites, and he says, "Every draft bait kid in this town should pull out his draft card right now, light it up, and say, "Hell no, I won't go." He lights up a small, white card, lets it burn down to almost nothing, and uses the end of the flame to light up a cigarette. "This whole town is going to be smoking on Saturday."

"Are you a student at this University?" A voice from a reporter.

"Don't I look like a student?" Hayden answers with a question of his own. "If it looks like a duck, quacks like a duck, it's probably a duck."

"Will this be a peaceful protest?" Another reporter asks.

"It's a peace march. What do you think?"

A few other questions are thrown Hayden's way, which he treats with the same ridicule. Jerk.

The picture switches back to the news anchors. "Seems like a friendly fellow," the male member of the newscast says with thick sarcasm.

"I bet he's a lot of fun at parties," the anchor lady adds.

"We'll be right back with Ace Dunnigan and sports after the break."

Half the pitcher is gone. I pour another glass. Every drunk at the bar is looking right at me, so I look back up at the TV. Of all people Diamond Jim is on the screen, "If it's insurance you need, see Diamond Jim Bradley."

The news comes back on.

"We have a live report from Ace Dunnigan. He's got some big, big news on the on-going Tony McIntyre saga. Ace..."

The shot flips to asshole Ace in front of the door to the Athletic Department. A slight bit of hesitation makes him look dumber than he already is. He starts talking, "Although the press wasn't allowed in the stadium this afternoon, I have confirmed that Touchdown Tony McIntyre was a no-show for the most important practice of the season. Touchdown Tony pulls a disappearing act two days before the State game. Unbelievable. Where is he? What is he doing? What could be more important than preparing for the game that can take the Pioneers to Pasadena? I've asked Coach Praytel, the assistant coaches, and a number of players, and all give me the same "No comment" answer. My sources tell me, 'Nobody has seen Tony and nobody knows where he is.' This news is on top of the rumors flying around that the Passing Pioneer is going back on his word to play out his senior year at Pioneer U, and entering the NFL draft. It's the last practice, before the biggest football Saturday, the University has seen in over twenty years, and Touchdown Tony McIntyre is nowhere to be found. I'll have more tonight at eleven. This is Ace Dunnigan live at the Athletic Department at Pioneer U. Back to you in the studio."

The anchor lady says, "Tony, Tony, where art thou, Tony?"

I drink the rest of the pitcher, out of the pitcher, and leave the bar.

By the time I get back to the American Legion, the parking lot is full. I have to park across the street in a muddy field.

The coffin has an American Flag draped over it, but you can still see the big dent. They set it up across from the bar on a small platform. There are two vases of flowers beside it, and an easel holding Jerry's picture. He's in uniform, but not smiling; maybe he knew something. Ruthie sits in a chair in front of the casket. She's crying.

The place is packed. A lot of men are in uniforms that no longer fit. I push through the crowd. A lot of people say stuff to me, but I ignore all comments. I get a few feet from Ruthie. Diamond Jim sits next to her, a cocktail and a huge plate of lasagna balanced on his lap. He's too busy eating and talking to notice me.

"The Legion would like to be there Saturday and give the salute."

Ruthie doesn't answer, just weeps.

"You should be proud. Jerry died a hero," Diamond Jim adds between bites.

"No, he didn't. He was killed by mortar that went off wrong." Ruthie manages to choke out.

"But he's a hero, none the less."

"I don't want a hero. I want my son."

Diamond Jim doesn't have a hand left to comfort her, so I quickly sit down on her other side, and put my arm around her. She cries on my shoulder.

"Where the hell have you been?" Diamond Jim asks me.

I don't bother to answer, but that doesn't stop more questions. "Is it true, you really going pro? You do that Tony, it will ruin the program for next year."

A Legionnaire, also balancing a plate, comes over and taps Jim on the shoulder. "Hurry up, there's only two pieces of lasagna left."

Diamond Jim waves him off. "You get me in the press box?"

"No."

"Why not?"

"That guy from the National Guard was a total asshole."

"That's not my fault."

"Tony," Ruthie says to me through her tears. "Why did my Jerry have to die?"

"I don't know."

"He didn't die for his country. Vietnam isn't near this country. What's in Vietnam that's so important my son has to die?"

"I wish I knew, Ruthie. I wish I knew."

My shoulder is soaked from her tears.

"Why didn't you show up today for practice?" Diamond Jim asks. "You're not hurt are you?"

130

"Not yet," I answer the fool.

Ruthie cries on my shoulder. Diamond Jim stuffs his face. Nobody gets near the casket. Whose idea was it to have a wake at a tavern? Ridiculous.

I'm mad, and I'm getting madder. The anger rising inside me is like a bruise swelling on your body. The beer, no doubt, helps fuel my negative emotions. This whole thing isn't right.

The so-called mourners are milling around, back-slapping. Nobody is somber. People are vying with big spoons to get the last bites of casseroles on the buffet table. The bar is three-deep with guys holding empty glasses up begging for a re-fill. People are greeting each other and laughing. At what, I can't imagine. Not one person in the place is wearing black. The place is filled with cigarette smoke. I can feel it when I breathe. A couple of old geezers come over and congratulate me for "Kicking that kid's ass off the stage." I ignore them. More guys are coming over, knowing Touchdown Tony is in their midst. Suddenly, all I can think about is getting out of the place. And that's when I see General August Brown. He's at the bar, dressed in his National Guard uniform, surrounded by a group of his military cronies. I rush over, butt right into the middle of the group, and come face to face with him.

"How much do you want?"

"What?" he says.

"How much do you want? I'll have at least three-hundred-grand after I'm drafted. You can have it all if you get me into the National Guard."

"What are you talking about kid?" He says, as the eyes of his buddies peer at him suspiciously.

"You know what I'm talking about. Courage you call it."

"You drunk kid?"

"No, are you?"

"I don't know what the hell you are talking about."

His face has turned bright red. He's sweating. The eyes of his buddies stay on him.

131

"I need to get in, and I need to get in now." I grip him by the medals on his chest and pull him up to me. "Is three-hundred grand enough courage for you?"

Brown squirms his little body back from me. I let go of his uniform. He's shaking, he's so scared. "I don't know what you're talking about kid, because I can't help you."

I lord over the little bastard like a lineman over a halfback. I should kick his ass.

One of his buddies asks me, as I'm staring down at the little weasel, "You're Touchdown Tony, aren't you?"

"I'm not so sure anymore."

I run out of the place like I'm crashing through a goal line stand. I knock a couple of jerks on their ass, but I could care less. I'm so angry, I forget where I parked the car. When I do find it, I climb inside, and my hand is shaking so badly, I can't get the key into the ignition. I pound on the steering wheel, eating up my energy, until I'm too exhausted to continue. I'm breathing as fast as I would after wind sprints.

Finally, I drive off, but there is no place I want to go.

**CHAPTER 17**

There are no chalk "chalk lines" on Astroturf, but I keep kicking on them, as if I can spread the white onto the green. I walk the perfect rectangle, around and around the field. The empty stands above me look as lonely as I feel. The press box, the only enclosed structure in the stadium, seems similar to a guard tower, rising above the prison yard where the inmates play. The tunnel in the corner of the end zone resembles a big, black tube; once you enter, you may never come out again. The picture of the Pioneer Mother, drawn on the fifty-yard line, has always seemed about as out of place as a woman in a locker room. The benches on the sidelines are empty. The goalposts stand alone. It is deathly quiet.

Football is the only thing in life I'm good at. I was born to play. My father not only passed along his genes, but taught me the game better than anyone ever could. And what he didn't know, my mother filled in. I can throw a perfect spiral sixty yards, and have it land on either the right or left shoulder of a receiver running at full speed. In a fraction of a second, my eyes can see the entire field, and pick out which receiver has a step on his defender. My brain signals to my arm the exact velocity, arc, angle, and trajectory of my pass, in a fraction of a fraction of a second. I run a 4.4 forty. I bench well over 300 pounds. I stand 6'4", weigh 220, and have 20-15 vision in both eyes. I'm praised. I'm adored. I'm sought after by everyone. Football wise, I'm perfect.

Without football, I'm nothing.

I have no education. I have no experience. I have no job skills. I'm not very smart. The only decisions I've ever made were on the field. I've never earned a paycheck. I've never had to find a friend. I've never owned a car, bought clothes, or did a chore. Every uniform I've ever worn has a big number on its back. I've had coaches on my sidelines, tutors at my schools, and trainers in the gym. People tell me where to go, what to do, and what to say.

As I pace around and around the lines, I try to imagine what my life will be without football, and in another uniform. I think of news stories of wounded soldiers being carried onto helicopters, the line-up of caskets in the plane delivering Jerry's remains, and soldiers coming back without arms and legs. Could it be me being wounded, or my remains in one of those caskets? And would anyone care? If I'm not playing quarterback, no one is going to give a shit about me.

I might not be too bright, but I'm not a fool. I can read—especially the writing on the wall.

It is well after midnight when I walk into the student union. An old black janitor sees me and gives me a *thumbs up*.

I smile, but don't speak.

I walk slowly down the long hallway, passing all the student association offices. The door to the SDS office is closed. I try to enter, but the door is locked. I knock. I wait. I knock again. I can hear noises inside. I knock for the third time, and the door opens.

"You're Touchdown Tony?" the kid, who couldn't be more than sixteen, asks.

"Is Molly around?"

"Huh?"

"Is Molly around?" I repeat. "The girl who sells the t-shirts."

"I haven't seen her."

I faintly hear a guitar. I push by the kid and follow the sound into the big room where all the work is done. The floor is wall-to-wall bodies; most are in sleeping bags, some with only a blanket. The room smells of body odor, dirty, wet clothes, and remnants of marijuana smoke. No wonder the door was locked. Marcus is in the far corner, alone, strumming the strings, and gently singing some song I don't recognize.

"Hey?"

Marcus stops the music. "Kinda late for tutoring, Tony."

"You got that right," I agree with him, more than he realizes.

Marcus doesn't look good. He's tired, worn, exhausted, like he's had the flu for a week. "What's the matter?" I ask.

134

He keeps strumming as he speaks. "Ever go into a game when you knew you were going to lose, worse yet, knew you were going to get slaughtered?"

"Once."

"What did you do?"

"I didn't do anything."

"You just went in there and got the crap beat out of you?"

"No. My mom told the coach I was hurt and couldn't play."

"So the backup QB got the shit kicked out of him?"

"Yeah."

"Was it hard to watch?"

"Not really, I stayed in the locker room most of the game."

"Well," Marcus says, "I don't think I have that option."

I sit down next to him. "I thought they cancelled the march."

"No, it's going to be bigger and better than ever."

"Just stay home."

"Can't do that," Marcus says.

"If you're going to get hurt, it'll be dumb to be there."

"Getting hurt is the least of my problems, Tony."

"Well then, change the march, do it at another time, or do it someplace else?"

"Game's already started, Tony. Can't stop it now."

"Don't do it if it's going to be a disaster," I tell him.

"Some things you just have to do."

"Why?"

"Because it's the right thing to do."

We sit for a moment. Marcus retunes his guitar. I'll never talk him out of the march. Why would he listen to me? He's the teacher, and I'm the idiot.

"You know where that Molly girl is?" I ask him.

"Try the storeroom," he says. "She's been sleeping in there since Hayden started doing Katie in the office."

I stand. Marcus doesn't glance up at me. I put out my hand. Now, he looks up. We shake hands, but don't exchange a word. I walk away slowly.

I step over and around bodies to get to the storeroom in the opposite corner. The door is open. I walk into the room. I kick an empty Coke bottle on the floor, and it knocks another six down in the process. My eyes adjust to the darkness, and I see there are two sleeping bags on the floor filling up the small space. There are two people in each bag. It is hard to see faces, but when I do, I'm embarrassed to see all faces are male. I hustle out of the room before one of the boys awakens.

I run out of the SDS offices high-stepping the maze of bodies, quicker than two lines of tires on the training field. Outside, the damp air feels good, because it's clean. I walk slowly back to the house.

Nobody's around. It's Thursday night. No doubt, everybody has already passed out after drinking too much. I go into my room.

My bed is occupied.

"How'd you get in here?" I ask her.

"I learned a long time ago how to get into places," Molly tells me.

I take off my coat, hang it on the hook, kick off my boots, sit on the desk chair, and put my feet up on the edge of the bed. Molly props herself up on the pillow.

"I saw Marcus."

"Yeah," she says. "He's not having a real good time."

"He said the whole march has gone bullshit on him, and people who show up are going to get beaten to a pulp."

"He's probably right."

"I told him to stay home."

"No, that's not going to happen," Molly says.

"I tried to convince him, but he wouldn't listen to me."

"If you want to see purity in the cause, you don't have to look much further than Marcus."

I look at her. She looks at me.

"I talked to Schwartz."

"Yeah."

"I offered him a hell of a deal."

"Yeah?"

"He blew me off, said he was too busy to talk about football. We're right in the middle of the season, on our way to the Rose Bowl, and he's *too busy*? I couldn't believe it."

"Everybody has their priorities, Tony."

I let out a big sigh. "I can't believe this is happening. This isn't right. Stuff like this isn't supposed to happen to people like me. I don't want to go into the Army, go to Vietnam, and shoot anybody. Who would?"

"You might ask your next door neighbor that question," Molly says pointing in the direction of Steve's room.

"I can't believe I was so stupid."

"You're not stupid, Tony. I know stupid, and you're not it."

I rest my head in my hands. "Schwartz was my last shot. I don't know what to do next."

"What's the right thing to do?"

"I don't know. Somebody has got to tell me."

I sit in the chair, pull the curtains back, and stare out the window into the night. I feel emotions I can't remember ever having. Molly pulls the covers to the side. "Get undressed, Tony. Come to bed. It's after two in the morning. Nothing is going to happen right now."

I get up slowly, strip off my clothes, and climb into bed. I lie on my back, spread my right arm under her. She rests on my shoulder, her face facing mine. "I'm scared, Molly I'm really, really scared."

For the first time, in more years than I can remember, a tear falls from my eye.

Molly wipes the tear away with her hand. "It's okay."

And I don't stop at one tear. One after another after another, a cascade of emotion empties out of my eyes, down my cheeks, and onto my chest. I can't stop. It feels like something has died inside of me, and has to drain out ever so slowly. It hurts in a way I've never been hurt before.

"Let it all out, Tony. Let it all come out," Molly coaches me, as she wipes the moisture off my face.

The big, bad, Heisman Trophy candidate weeps like a two-year-old child.

"What am I going to do?" I finally am able to mutter.

"You just have to go on, believe that it's all going to work out, and do what your heart tells you," she says. "I know it's tough, but that's all you can do."

**CHAPTER 18**

For the first time in my life, I sleep with a girl and don't have sex.

I wake well after nine. Oddly enough, I do feel a bit better. I don't get out of bed. Molly is still asleep. I reach over for Marcus' Vietnam book, pick it up, and continue reading. There is some arguing next door, which wakes Molly.

"Good morning."

"Let's hope so," I say, with a slight positive in my attitude.

The voices from next door get louder; it's Cindy and Steve. A door slams and the sounds stop.

Molly tucks herself into my body and holds me.

"If I enlist for four years, I wouldn't have to go to Vietnam."

"Really?"

I show her the passage from the book.

"Aren't you avoiding the issue?" she asks.

"What issue?"

"Whether you should or shouldn't go to Vietnam."

"Enlisting and getting drafted are the only choices I have."

"That's not true."

"It isn't?"

"You don't have to go, if you don't want to, Tony."

"You think I can become a Conscientious Objector?"

"No," she says. "You lost that option when you beat up the protestor on TV."

"Then what other choices do I have?"

"Don't go," Molly says.

"What do you mean, 'Don't go'?"

"Split to Canada."

"I can't do that."

"Why not?"

"I've never been to Canada."

"I've never been to Montana, but that wouldn't stop me from

going," Molly explains.

"Canada?"

"I'll go with you. I got nothing better to do."

"What would we do up there?"

"I don't know. We'll find something. I don't know what, but we'll find something."

I hesitate.

"You know, Tony," Molly says. "You getting drafted may be a good thing."

I look at her like she's crazy.

"Force you to make your own decisions. Get off on your own. Find out what Tony McIntyre is really made of."

I want to argue, but she won't let me.

"When you find yourself in a crisis, you find out who you really are."

"I know who I am, Molly. I'm a Heisman Trophy candidate."

"That's not who you are, that's what people want you to be. I'm not even sure if that's what you want to be. Try challenging yourself, Tony, and not on a football field, or in bed with a woman, or dropping clichés in front of a TV camera. Do something on your own." She pauses. "You don't know what you can do, Tony, until you try to do something you don't think you can do."

I don't respond.

"I left home when I was a sophomore in high school. I lived on the streets for six months. I ate out of dumpsters, slept in abandoned buildings, snuck into the Y to take a shower. I did some things I'm not proud of. Finally, I found a job and a room to live in. It worked out. I survived. If I can do it, Tony, so can you."

"It's different for you than it would be for me," I tell her.

"Why?"

"Because you're not Touchdown Tony McIntyre."

"And maybe neither are you anymore."

"Don't say that."

"The reality is you could be wearing a new uniform in a couple of weeks. Forget about football. Start considering your life.

What's in your heart? What do you believe in? What is the best course for Tony McIntyre's life? Whatever those are, you can perform and achieve them on a much bigger stage than some college football stadium. I believe in you, Tony, and I'd believe in you a lot more if you'd start believing in yourself."

A knock comes on the door. "Tony, are you in there?"

"What?"

Steve, in his ROTC uniform, enters my room. "Tony?"

Before I have a chance to answer, Steve sees Molly. "You again?"

"Soldier boy, oh my little soldier boy," Molly sings to him.

"What's going on, Tony? Everybody's worried about you."

"Trust me," Molly says to Steve. "Nobody is more worried about him than him."

"I didn't ask you," Steve says to Molly.

"Why do you have your uniform on? It's not Tuesday." I interrupt the pending fight.

"They're calling us out tomorrow, along with the National Guard. If those hippie freaks make me miss the game, I'm going to make target practice out of each and every one of them."

"That's a pleasant thought," Molly says.

Steve looks like an idiot in his uniform. He stands at attention over by the window.

"Was that Cindy I heard leaving this morning?" I ask.

"Yeah."

"You finally have sex with her."

"No."

For the first time in days, I want to laugh.

"She'd decided she'll sleep in the same bed with me, but won't do me."

I laugh, so does Molly.

"It's not funny."

I laugh some more, so does Molly.

"Oh, shit," Steve says, looking out the window. "Look who's here."

I twist my body around, push the curtain to the side, and see a van pull up, and double-park in front of the house. On the side of the van is a big Channel 7 TV logo and the words, *Seven's on your Side*.

"Let me handle this," Steve says, and rushes from the room.

We both get out of bed. Molly puts on one of my sweatshirts. I pull on a t-shirt. Outside, Ace Dunnigan, a guy holding a camera, and a guy holding a small box emerge from the van. Steve meets them on the lawn. I crank my window open to hear.

Ace asks, "Where's Tony?"

Steve answers, "He's not here."

"I don't believe you."

"I don't care."

"His car's here," Ace makes a good point.

"Well, he isn't."

"You're a lousy liar," Ace tells Steve.

"I am not. I'm an excellent liar," Steve counters.

"We're coming in."

"No, you're not."

Ace brushes past Steve.

I take one of the trophies off the shelf, and heave it out the window. It misses Ace by about two feet, crashes onto the walkway, and shatters into pieces. My next trophy misses by only a foot. I duck back behind the curtain, so Ace can't see me. Molly hands me the next trophy, and this one hits the camera the guy is holding. Steve covers his head and runs for cover. I throw another. It's raining monuments of memorabilia.

One more toss and I have the reporter and crew on the run. I fling my framed pictures and plaques like Frisbees. Two hit the side of the van. I hope my aim is this good tomorrow. As Molly hands me the last memento/projectile, Ace dives into the van's front seat, and the vehicle streaks down the street. Game over.

Three minutes later, Steve is back upstairs, carrying what's left of my past football career.

"What the hell are you doing?" he asks out of breath.

142

"I missed practice yesterday. I thought I'd get in some work this morning."

"You win the Super Bowl, Tony, these could be worth some real money," Steve chokes out.

"Keep 'em. They're yours."

Steve must believe he's got a hell of a deal, because he hustles out of the room and back into his. As he does, I go to the closet, pull my one tie off the rack, carry it to the door, hang it on the outside knob, and close the door.

I return to the room, take Molly in my arms, and hold her. Her warmth pulses through my body faster than a sideline heater. I pull back, kiss her ever so gently, and whisper to her, "Thank you."

We embrace, and gently kiss again. For these few moments, my troubles melt away. I pull the sweatshirt from her body, lay her down on the bed, and we gently caress each other before we become truly intimate.

This is heaven.

The door crashes open so hard, the knob cracks the plaster on the back wall.

"What the hell are you doing?"

"Mom."

My mother bursts into the room like a power fullback through a weak defensive line.

"You don't have sex the day before a game!"

"Why not?" Molly asks.

"Who the hell are you?" Mom asks.

Molly sticks her right hand out from under the covers. "Hi, I'm Molly, nice to meet you."

Mom takes her hand and yanks her out of bed. "Get the hell out of here, you little whore."

"She's not a whore," I scream at my mother.

"She's looks like a whore to me."

"No, I'm not a whore," Molly says now on her feet. "I used to be, but I'm not anymore."

Mother pulls her farther away from the bed. "Get your clothes, get your ass, and get the hell out of here."

"So, I'm guessing this is a bad time for us to chat and get to know each other?" Molly says.

My mother slaps her across the face. Molly goes down. I jump out of bed and get between Molly and my mother. "What the hell are you doing?"

"Get her out of here."

I pick Molly off the floor.

Molly is shaken, trying to get her balance back. "It's okay, Tony."

"Get the bitch out of here." My mother spits out venomously.

I try to hold Molly, but she breaks free. "It's okay," she reassures me, as she scrambles to put on her clothes.

I face my mom. "You don't hit the woman I love, Mother!"

Molly freezes. Her mouth drops open as she stares at me.

I turn, and my mother slaps me harder than I've ever been hit, and I've been hit pretty damn hard in my life.

Mom screams at Molly, "I said, get the hell out of here."

I feel the welt across my cheek immediately swell.

Molly's trying to find her clothes.

"Mother."

"Shut up."

Mom is pushing Molly, who is pulling on her jeans and top. "Get the hell out of here."

Molly looks at me, tears in her eyes beginning to well up.

I'm on the bed, hand against my face. I look at Molly, but I don't move.

Mom pushes her out the door, "Out!"

The door slams. My mother turns back to me. The fire burns in her eyes.

"What are you doing?" I scream at my mother. "I love that girl."

"Love, what the hell do you know about love?"

"More than you think I know," I yell back.

144

"You think you know about love; you don't know anything," she tells me.

"Yes, I do."

"No, you don't. How could you? You don't even know enough to follow simple directions."

"Maybe if you'd let me."

"Are you kidding?"

"No."

My mom stands over me like my old Pop Warner football coach used to do when he wanted to intimidate me. "What the hell are you doing, Tony?"

"I told you never to come here."

"You don't tell me what to do." She comes at me again with a raised hand. I put up my wrists to deflect the blow, but she backs off.

She looks down at me like I'm deformed. "How the hell can you be so damned stupid?"

I cover up my naked body.

"You missed practice yesterday."

I didn't feel..."

"You flunk out of this worthless institution."

"I missed a..."

"You get drafted into the Army?"

Shit.

She's on me like I'm a six-year-old again. "You think I enjoyed driving you to games and workouts and camps all over creation? You think I liked freezing my butt off sitting on rotting benches in crumbling high school stadiums? You think I catered to your every need and whim for the last twenty years, so I could see my only son wearing Army fatigues?"

"How'd you know?"

"You think I'm stupid too?" She asks. "I know everything, Tony. It's my business to know."

The only time I've ever seen her like this was when I threw two interceptions in a row in high school. I thought she was going to have a coronary on the sideline, she was so angry.

"And why the hell didn't you call me?" she asks.

"I thought I could work it out myself."

"You thought?" She comes closer to me. "You thought?"

"I've been thinking a lot. About me, about Vietnam..."

"You're thinking?"

"Yes."

"You, who aren't smart enough to stay in school? You, who are whoring around the day before a game? You, who missed practice yesterday? You, who tells Praytel you're blowing off your senior year? You're thinking?"

"Yes, I..."

"You want to think about something, Tony? Think about the most important game of your life, think about a career in the NFL, think about your father, and the tradition you have to fulfill. Is that enough to fill your head, Tony?"

I lie on the bed like a helpless child, forced to take some very strong medicine.

"Stop thinking. Can you do that? Can you just stop thinking?"

I speak very softly. "I have to report for my physical in ten days."

"No, you don't."

"Yes, I do."

"No, you don't."

"I got this letter in the mail."

"Listen to me."

"I went to the draft board."

"Shut up, Tony. You don't have to go."

"What?"

"It's all fixed," she tells me. "Justice got you into an Army Reserve unit in Texas."

I can't believe I'm hearing what I'm hearing.

"It'll probably cost us half your signing bonus, but I didn't have much of a choice."

I rub the side of my face.

146

She backs up slightly, but never takes her eyes off me. "Aren't you going to thank your mother?"

I hesitate.

"I didn't hear you."

"Thanks."

Mom leans on the edge of the built-in desk. "Now, you know what you're going to do?"

"No."

"First, you're going to stop thinking."

"Okay."

"Next, since you look terrible, you're going to get up and get dressed. I'm going to get some good food into you. We'll go to my hotel, where you're going to get some rest. You have to report to the team at four."

"Okay."

"And on Saturday, you only have to do one thing." Mom raises her index finger.

"What?"

"You have to show everybody Tony McIntyre is the best, damn, college quarterback in the nation."

## CHAPTER 19

"You have a responsibility, Tony," Mom tells me as we drive out of her hotel and across campus.

"What?"

"To me, to your father, but mostly to yourself."

I pull my hood up, so no one notices me in a car with my mother.

"Not only have you been given an incredible physical gift, you have been carefully trained, nurtured, and coached to use your God-given talent to the best of your ability. You realize that?"

"I guess so."

"You guess so? You better start doing a lot more than guessing, Tony. You're on the verge of greatness. You're the next Joe Namath. Only months from now, you'll be playing in front of hundreds of thousands of people every Sunday. You'll be rich, famous, the envy of every kid in America." She pauses to let it all sink in. "And all you have to do is be responsible for one thing."

"What?"

"Your talent."

I don't respond.

"It's your responsibility to respect your talent. That's all you have to do. Everything else will be taken care of. You'll have the best agent, coaches, financial people, all on your side, working for you. You won't have to worry about anything except playing up to your potential. You won't have to think, or decide, or deal with life's petty problems like everybody else in the world." She turns my way and gives me a smile. "You want to think about something, son? Think about how good you've got it."

She's right. I look out over the campus and see the banners hanging on the student union, my picture on posters spread all over campus. I see students lugging their books, hurrying to the last class of the week; it'll take them years to get what I've got guaranteed. Ninety-nine percent of them won't even come close.

They'll end up in some office job, or some dumb career they won't enjoy, and always be struggling to pay the rent, or worried that they'll get laid off. I should feel sorry for them, but I don't. Some wear sweatshirts with my picture on the front.

We arrive at the hotel a few minutes past four. The team has already arrived on the bus. Mom parks in the underground lot and we walk inside together. The players are milling around the lobby area. Some guys are talking to reporters. Some are eating. Some are playing slap ass with one another. Praytel and his coaches are scattered about the room.

We pass through the hallway and into the lobby area, and are met with blinding lights from a TV camera, shining into our eyes. A microphone is pushed into my face, and I hear, "Touchdown Tony, where the heck have you been?"

It's Ace Dunnigan.

Mom grabs his microphone, pushes it to the side, and uses her other hand to block the lens of the camera. "No comments, people," she shouts. "No comment."

Mother pulls me toward the rest of the team, who, when they see me, break into a round of applause. Praytel comes running up to us, shields Ace from getting any closer, and says to Mom, "Let's get him out of here."

A couple of my teammates slap me on the back, or give me five as we rush by. Praytel leads us into a small room off to the left of the registration desk. We step inside and an assistant coach guards the door from the outside.

"Nice of you to grace us with your presence, Tony," Praytel's words of welcome.

The room is small. There are three places to sit, but I don't.

"Where the hell have you been?" Praytel asks.

"What difference does it make?" Mom asks him.

"A lot," Praytel tells Mom. "He missed practice."

"You going to kick him off the team?"

"No."

"Then it doesn't make any difference," Mom says.

149

Praytel has no comeback.

"He's here. He's rested. He's ready to play," Mom says. "Let's just forget everything else."

"It's a bit hard to do."

"That's your problem, not ours."

Praytel is about to speak, but doesn't.

"I don't want him talking to the press, or having to explain himself to anyone," Mom orders. "From this point on, all we should be concerned with is the game. Forget everything else. Agreed?"

Praytel shakes his head and says, "Agreed, but he better be his old self, come tomorrow."

"Don't worry about Tony. He'll be the best."

"And he's going to listen to me?" Praytel asks.

"As long as you're calling a game that makes sense for his talents, you won't have a problem," Mom continues to speak for me.

"Right, Tony?" Praytel asks me for assurance.

I feel like a dummy on the hand of a ventriloquist. "Yeah."

Mom takes me aside. "I have to go back and pick up your father. Take it easy tonight. Don't talk to anyone. It's none of anyone's business what happened before. Don't let anyone give you a hard time." She reaches up and puts her right hand behind my head. "If you want to do any thinking, Tony, think about how you're going to shred those Woodchucks." She pulls my head down to her level and kisses me on my good cheek. "Tomorrow, you're going to show everyone what Touchdown Tony McIntyre is made of."

One of the assistant coaches escorts me past Ace, the rest of the press flunkies, and into the elevator. "You okay, Tony?" he asks after the doors shut and we're alone.

"I'm fine."

The coach leads me down the hall to #404. We enter. Arthur waits inside. The assistant coach leaves.

"My prayers were answered when you returned, just like the

150

prodigal son," Arthur tells me.

"Great. Thanks a bunch, Arthur."

---

The team meeting is at 4:45. We're in a big room. I sit in the back. A portable screen is set up on a riser in the front. We watch film of the Woodchuck's offense, and our Defensive Coordinator goes over how we plan to stop their run game, their passing game, and their special teams. Next, we watch film of their defensive alignments and Praytel goes over their strengths and weaknesses. This is boring. What is even more boring is when Praytel outlines his offensive, game plan. The same dumb, run and shoot, ten to fifteen yard, one side to the other, blah, blah, blah, do it the Praytel way, so-called attack. If I'm going to shine in this game, I'm going to have to throw the ball more than ten yards.

Dinner's at the hotel. It's steak, baked potatoes, green beans, salad, and rolls. Arthur says grace. I've never heard this one before. He probably wrote it himself. We can have as much as we want, and a lot of guys double up on the meat. Lester starts farting before dessert, which is pudding. I hate pudding. I ask for some ice cream and I get two scoops of vanilla.

After dinner we get our big treat. We don't have to watch some movie so old it's in black and white. They screen *The Wild Bunch*, a big hit movie of the year. It's the story of this old gang of criminals trying to steal gold, but they get double-crossed, set-up, and end up fighting a bunch of Mexicans in a wild shootout at the end of the movie. Not only is someone getting slaughtered almost every minute of the movie, but the film leaves nothing to the imagination when it comes to getting shot up by rifles, pistols, and even a machine gun. There is more blood and guts on the screen than a Vietnam news story. Arthur can't take it. He walks out, but I don't go that far. I close my eyes during the real gory parts. The rest of the team really gets into it. The boys are whooping it up, shouting, and doing body counts as people are sliced and diced on the screen. The movie makes me sick.

---

It's around eleven. We're lying in bed on our backs, staring at the ceiling. We each know each other is awake, but remain quiet. After a few minutes Arthur asks, "Are you nervous, Tony?"

"About losing?"

"Yeah."

"No."

"Really?"

"All I have to do is play well. If I play well and we lose, I still played well. I play well and we win, all the better."

"I'm nervous," he admits.

"About what?

"The game."

"What about the game?"

"What if I fumble, miss a block, drop a pass, and we lose the game?"

"I don't know."

"I can't believe you're not nervous," he says.

"I'm not."

"I am."

"Pray some more."

"If God hasn't heard me by now, Tony, he must be too busy to listen."

There is a short pause in our conversation.

"This is your last chance for a bowl game, isn't it?" I ask, knowing this is his senior year.

"These last games are pretty much my final hymn."

"What are you going to do when you graduate?"

"I've been accepted at Princeton Divinity."

"What's that?"

"The top of the ladder graduate school, when it comes to becoming a minister."

"You don't have to go in the Army?"

"No. High draft number."

Another few quiet moments.

"There's been a lot of rumors floating around about you," Arthur tells me.

"There's always a lot of rumors about me. It comes with being the quarterback."

"Did you really get drafted?"

"Not yet, but I will, into the NFL."

"You're not coming back to Pioneer U?"

"No."

"Is that what you want?"

"Who wouldn't?"

"Me."

"You're telling me, you wouldn't want to get drafted into the NFL, get a huge signing bonus, a four or five year guaranteed contract, and make more money than you ever dreamed?"

"Yes," Arthur says, "this road is pretty much run its course. Time to move on, do something different, try something new. That's why I hope I don't make a mistake in the game, and end my football career in shame."

"Then you better keep praying."

"I will," he says. "I'll pray for you too."

I pause.

"What are you going to say to God about me, Arthur?"

"That you do whatever's right at the exact right time you do it."

"I guess that's a good idea," I say.

"You ever pray, Tony?"

"No, I've never been much on praying."

"You might want to give it a go. It can't hurt," he says and rolls on his side facing away from me.

"Goodnight, Arthur."

"Goodnight, Tony. And go Pioneers."

153

I lie quietly for a few more minutes and think about praying, but I don't. I roll onto my side, close my eyes, and go to sleep.

## CHAPTER 20

Game days are rituals. I, and every one of my teammates, follow a personal ritual.

I get up at nine, shower, take a good crap, pull on a pair of sweats, turn on the TV, and watch cartoons. I never read a newspaper, or watch a news show on TV. At 9:45, I go downstairs to have breakfast with the team. I always have three eggs, a banana, a stack of pancakes, and two large glasses of orange juice. After breakfast, I have to sit through one of Praytel's *Fire us up* pep talks, which bores the hell out of me. At eleven, I'm back up in the room. I put on my slacks, white shirt, tie, and green sports coat. At 11:30, we board the bus to the stadium. I always sit as far away from Praytel as possible.

Today, my routine is interrupted.

I'm coming out of the shower with only a towel around me. Arthur is going in. A knock comes on our door. I look at Arthur. He looks at me. I answer the door.

"How'd you get up here?"

"I told you I know how to get into hotel rooms," she says as she enters.

Arthur is embarrassed and hurries into the bathroom.

"How are you?" Molly asks taking a seat on the edge of Arthur's bed.

"I'm okay."

"Sure was nice meeting your Mom, yesterday. I bet she's a real riot in her weekly bridge game."

I move away from her to the back of the room where my suitcase is. I pull out a pair of sweats and carefully slip them on. The towel doesn't come off until I'm covered.

"Tony..."

I don't let her get started. "It's done."

"What's done?"

"It's over. I'm out of the draft. My agent got me into a reserve unit in Texas. I'm going into the NFL. The problem's solved."

"What problem?" she asks.

"Me getting drafted."

"What about everything else?" she asks.

"There isn't anything else."

"You've got bigger problems than just getting out of the draft, Tony."

"Not anymore, I don't."

Molly sits on the bed and gives me an odd stare, as if she's not hearing what I'm telling her. "You sure?"

"Yes."

"You think this through?"

I get a bit animated. I don't like this conversation. I want it to end. "I'm sick of thinking. I've thought enough. It's only gotten me in trouble. All I want to do is play football. That's all I care about."

Molly stands, but doesn't move toward me. "So, you put on number 12, and everything is going to be perfect again?"

"Yes."

"I don't think so."

"Then you should quit thinking."

"You can't go back to who you were. You learned too much," Molly tells me. "You have to start being who you are."

"What I am is a football player. One of the best there is. I'm a Heisman Trophy candidate. This is all I have ever been and all I ever wanted to be."

"You're much more than that."

"I'm the next Joe Namath, and that's enough for anyone."

"I don't think so."

"Then quit thinking."

Molly turns toward me and speaks from her heart. "It's not enough for the Tony I know."

"Don't say that."

She starts to move towards me. "So, you go out, get on the field, throw a couple of touchdowns, win the big game, and pretend last week never happened?"

I don't have an answer.

"Even if you win today, you lose, Tony."

"Forget last week. It doesn't matter. All that matters is showing America that Tony McIntyre is the best college quarterback in the nation."

"You really believe that?"

"Yes."

"No, you don't."

"Quit telling me what I think!" I scream at her.

"Why not? Everybody else does."

"Just forget about last week," I continue to scream.

"You can't," she says, "and neither can I."

I back up, but there is no place to go in the room where she can't see me.

"You finally got a taste of what you're capable of, and you're scared."

"No, I'm not."

"Instead of being the next Joe Namath today, try being the next Tony McIntyre."

"I don't have to anymore. The problem is gone."

"The problem is bigger than ever," she says.

"You're just one of them; you just want a piece of me like everybody else."

"I do," she says. "I want a piece of your heart."

I can barely breathe.

Molly is next to me. She places her hand on my heart. "Are you going to forget about loving me too? I thought I heard you say…"

"I didn't mean it." I interrupt her before she can say the words.

Molly's bottom lip starts to quiver. She's unsteady on her feet. A small tear falls from her eye.

"I was all screwed up last week. I didn't know what to think. I'm sorry if I told you something I didn't really mean."

She stands, and stares into my eyes for what seems like an

eternity. "I'm sorry," she finally says.

"It wasn't your fault."

"Yes, it was," she says. "I made a mistake."

I see tears falling from her eyes as she walks slowly around the bed, past where I stand, opens the door, says, "I thought I found someone I could believe in. I was wrong."

Molly leaves the room.

Arthur comes out of the bathroom, sees me standing in the corner. He's about to speak, but doesn't. He might be saying a prayer. The silence is uncomfortable. Arthur walks to the nightstand between the beds, and flips on the radio.

The next voice we hear comes out of the small speaker. "It's going to be an absolutely beautiful day for a civil war."

## CHAPTER 21

I never have my eggs scrambled, but I do today because they'll be easier to get down. My stomach is in knots. The orange juice makes it even queasier. I pour way too much syrup on the pancakes, take one bite, and push the plate away. I get the banana down and maybe half of the eggs, but that's all. I can feel my insides ready to explode.

And I'm not alone. The whole team is jumpy. I see forks dropped, juice spilled, food sliding off plates. Some guys over eat game day; some hardly eat at all. Few will admit it, but they're nervous. Some are quick to argue; some can't sit still. Most can't concentrate. I see a couple of them shake a bit. No matter if it's high school, college, or the pros, the crappers in locker rooms, on game day, always do double duty.

Praytel isn't helping. After we eat or don't eat, he gets up and starts spouting about honor, pride, and responsibility. What the hell does he know about honor and pride? Give me a break. He talks about how each of us knows exactly what we have to do, how to do it, and now it's time to perform. "There's no room for less than 100% effort, no place for second best, and no excuses for failure."

Praytel tells the offensive line to "hit them harder than they hit you." He tells the defensive line to "tackle them, so they know they've been tackled." He tells the receivers to "watch the damn ball go into their hands," and he tells the defensive backs to stay on their receivers like "stink on shit." "And Tony," he says to me, "you owe it to this team to give them the bowl game they deserve, to lead them to a victory they can remember the rest of their lives. You're the leader, the heart and soul, the one who can make the difference between victory and defeat. The team trusts you will carry out the game plan, on the field, where the game will be won. Every man on this team, every fan in the stands, and every student at this university is counting on you, Tony McIntyre.

I believe, and the team believes, you won't let us down."

What a load of crap. You know how many times I've heard this speech? It never changes, different coaches, different places, different times, same old, same old, same old crap. The only positive of listening to this idiot is it takes my mind off Molly. Why'd she have to show up today? She knows how important this game is. I told her about the Rose Bowl, and what a game like this can do for me. She couldn't have waited until tomorrow or at least after the game? Why'd she have to show up this morning? I've had enough distractions in the past week to last me a lifetime. I didn't need hers this morning.

The more I consider Molly, the more I realize Mom was right. Molly is hardly the woman for me. We come from different worlds. We want different things. She has a history behind her. My God, she slept with Hayden, and how could she ever expect me to get past that? Molly and I would never make it. Who was I kidding?

Once I'm in the NFL, I'll have more women than I know what to do with. And it won't be a lot of prissy co-eds, but hot models, actresses, and women right out of the center of *Playboy*. Why would I want to waste my best years tied down to one woman? There's no way I'd ever stay faithful. No red-blooded, young, dynamic athlete could say "No" to beautiful women throwing themselves at their feet. Why would I be any different?

Praytel keeps talking and talking and talking. He takes a deep breath, pauses, and says, "Winning isn't one thing—winning is everything," and Praytel finally shuts up and sits down. The end.

Nobody applauds, cheers, or acknowledges any change in their mood. I hear one of the players behind me whisper, "That was riveting." And another say, "My high school freshman coach gave better pep talks than that one." My sentiments exactly.

Praytel stands up, and every guy on the teams is saying to himself, "Oh please, no more. Please."

Praytel says, "And we have a special guest today. You all know him as a man who has done more for the Pioneer Football program than anyone. A supporter, benefactor, a mentor to you all. Let's give a big welcome to the head of the Pioneer Athletic Alumni Football Program, Mr. Eugene Swallow."

Marcus walks out the kitchen door.

"My name is Marcus Jones, and I'm here to ask the team for your support."

Praytel is too stupid to realize what is going on and starts to stutter, "Who the hell are you?"

Marcus ignores Praytel. I wish I could do the same. He continues, "There is going to be a march on campus today for peace. It's important we're not only heard, but supported by the Pioneer community. I ask for you, before the game begins today, to stand in silence for one minute." Marcus raises his hands in peace signs. "Put two fingers into the air as a sign of peace, and show the world the war in Vietnam is pointless, unjust, and a waste of human life."

"What the hell you doing, boy?" Eugene Swallow comes out from the other side of the room, grabs Marcus by the shirt collar and yanks him from where he stood. "You don't talk to my team about your anti-war bullshit..."

Marcus tries to reply, but Eugene whips him around, throws him on the floor, and continues his rant, "especially on game day, you little piece of shit."

One of the assistant coaches joins the fray. Marcus is down and unprotected. Mr. Swallow wails on him with both his fancy shoes, landing kick after kick. As the coach lifts Marcus up to toss him through the swinging doors, Eugene Swallow lands one last punch to his ribs, which doubles Marcus up. I hear the air go out of him like a bike tire going flat.

I'm standing with the rest of the team watching the slaughter, and just for an instant, Marcus looks up and catches my eye. I look away.

Eugene gladly helps toss Marcus into the kitchen, as if he's a bag of trash, and storms back into the room. The man has the fire of Satan in his eyes. He's so hyped, he's frantic. Praytel should suit

161

him up.

"And that's what you've got to do to those Woodchucks today," Eugene screams at the team. "You got to kick the living shit out of them!"

The entire team, with the exception of Arthur and me, explode into cheers.

"You're not on that field to win, you're there to destroy. Break them physically, mentally, and emotionally. Leave no doubt whatsoever that you are not only the best, but the best they will ever know. Hit them so hard, they'll lose all confidence in the belief they can win. Hurt them so bad, they'll feel the pain all the way into next season. Beat them so bad, the only feeling they will leave the field with is ultimate humiliation."

We might as well be in the front row at the Roman Coliseum. It's madness. Guys are screaming, swearing, hurling hatred at maximum decibel levels. Dirty dishes hit the floor. Drinks are thrown. Fists pound on tables. Lester is especially animated, howling like a coyote after a kill. Guys are bouncing into each other like sumo wrestlers. Eyes are blazing. Mouths are frothing. This is nuts.

"And that's what I want to see on the field today!" Eugene sums it up.

There is one more outburst of absolute venom. Praytel comes to the center of the room, raises his hands and yells out, "Now get upstairs, get dressed, and get packed. The bus leaves in thirty minutes."

And it's over. It just stops, like someone flipped the off switch, the balloon deflated, or the TV program goes to a commercial. No more screaming, emotion, or bluster. The players file out of the room, into the hallway, and onto the elevators. I don't move. I stand at a table alone. The bus boys come out to clean up the mess. Waiters return chairs to the edges of the tables. Praytel is slapping Eugene Swallow on the back. I consider heading for the kitchen and try to find Marcus, but instead I sit back down. For some reason, it all doesn't make any sense. A bad

162

pep talk and a few screamed epithets of hatred and we turn into animals? What the hell was Marcus trying to prove? It was stupid for him to be here, but why did they have to beat him up? If my stomach was tied up before breakfast, it's got knots in it now no Boy Scout could ever untangle.

Arthur is already In the room when I get back upstairs. "You okay, Tony?" He asks as he sees me come in the door.

"I'm fine."

"Why does everybody have to swear so much?" Arthur asks. "Is using the Lord's name in vain so necessary the coaches can't give a speech without it?"

"A couple more games, Arthur, and you won't have to listen to it anymore."

"Thank God."

I retrieve my equipment bag from the closet, put it on my bed, and start tossing my stuff inside. I take off my sweats, tennis shoes and socks, and toss them in too. I go back into the closet, grab the hanging bag, unzip it, pull my hard shoes out of the bottom, and the three hangers from the top. I lay them all on the bed.

This is my first uniform of the day: black shoes, tan slacks, white shirt, gold tie, and a green sports coat. It will be a day of uniforms. The next one I'll wear will have pads to protect my shoulders, hips, and ribs; a helmet with a steel bar to protect my face; and a jersey with the number 12 on the back and front. I'll uniform from preppy college boy, to weekend warrior, and back to preppy college boy, all in a matter of hours.

I'm dressed. Arthur's dressed. My bag's packed and so is his. I'm ready to leave, but not Arthur. Facing the bed, he gets down on his knees, laces his fingers together, and rests his forearms on the sheets. Before closing his eyes, he asks, "Care to join me?"

"No thanks."

I watch Arthur's lips slightly move, but not speak. I stay perfectly still. I ask myself why? What's the point? Why ask for help? The only thing you need going into a game is a belief in yourself. If you believe you're the best, you'll be the best. You'll perform at your highest level because you have the talent, the guts, and you're not afraid of anything. If something stands in your way, you push it aside and carry on.

He's finished. We grab our bags and head downstairs to the bus.

Most of the team is already in the parking lot. There are always a few tardy idiots, probably because they haven't learned to tell time. I hear someone mention there's going to be a line-up of fans along our route to the stadium, cheering us on our way. Oh, boy. The cheerleaders are here, but no band; thank God. Relatives, girlfriends, fans, and hangers-on are spread around the bus, and, to my surprise, I see my parents. Mom stands behind Dad's wheelchair at the edge of the crowd.

"What are you doing here?" I ask approaching the pair.

"Dad and I wanted to wish you the best," Mom says.

I should say "Thanks," but I don't.

"This is your day, Tony," Mom says. "This is the day you prove to the world you're the best there is, and the best that will ever be."

I should respond, but I don't. What would be the point?

"Your destiny starts today, Tony."

Dad reaches up with his good arm, takes mine and pulls me down to him. "Make me proud, son," he says as loud as he can, but I can barely hear him.

"Thanks, Dad. I'll do my best."

I give his arm a slight squeeze, smile, and raise up. The moment I'm standing erect, Mom throws her arms around me, hugs me, and kisses the side of my face. She knows she's embarrassing me, but doesn't care. Pulling back, she pats me on my chest and says. "Now you go out there today and shred those Woodchucks."

"Sure, Mom."

I hurry onto the bus, and find a seat in the back, next to a window.

Praytel is the last one to board. He sits in the front row. The driver closes the door, and the bus begins to move.

**CHAPTER 22**

The route is the same. North a few miles, turn left, up the street past the frat house, right on University where the cemetery borders the campus, continue past the athletic fields and the old basketball arena, cross 13$^{th}$ at the student union, go across campus, over the highway, into the parking lot, and up to the tunnel, where we'll unload and make our way into the locker room. Twenty minutes max.

The bus is one of those tourist busses, a big one with a bathroom in the back. It's higher than a regular city or school bus, and has tinted windows so we can see out, but it's hard to see in. I sit three rows from the back.

It's quiet, not a lot of talking going on.

This Saturday is different. For one, it's sunny. We don't get many sunny days this time of year. Two, it's crowded. There are cars everywhere. This town doesn't get traffic, but it's got it today. Stoplights are twelve to fifteen cars deep. Horns honk in frustration. There's no parking; I haven't seen an empty spot yet. Even the side streets are filled with cars, which can't seem to move. It doesn't make sense. If you're coming for the game, you're way too early, and you wouldn't park on this side of town, because the walk to the stadium is way too far.

People are heading for the campus, but it's not a football crowd. There are hippies with their long hair, bums, derelicts, scruffy sorts, but also parents with children, high school kids, and normal, everyday middle class folk with two cars in the garage and 2.3 kids in the family. Some carry signs and placards. Some wear an article of clothing displaying the American flag. A few smoke dope. Many carry one flower. I've never seen a crowd like this on campus, or any other place for that matter.

As the bus slowly makes its way, I see the frat house where a number of cars I don't recognize are parked on the front lawn. The brothers are outside talking with a group of mostly older guys who unload cases of beer from the back of a pick-up truck. This older group wear black jackets with *America, Love It or Leave It* stenciled on the back.

I see in the distance, the University corner, where the bus will turn to go onto campus. There, big crowds of people swarm into the street. One group, who line up on the athletic field side of the street, is dressed in the green and gold colors of the day; many wear Pioneer sweatshirts with my image on the front. As we approach, these fans cheer us onto victory. On the opposite corner, the Pioneer Band, in full regalia, waits impatiently. Thank God, they're not playing. As the bus makes the turn, the band bumps into each other like errant pinballs, trying to get into place, and follow the bus on its way to the stadium. A little farther down the street, a black hearse is illegally parked in front of the cemetery walkway.

As the bus creeps along, another set of uniforms catch my eye. In the right hand corner of the cemetery an honor guard begins to line up alongside an open grave. Diamond Jim, who is three sizes too big for the blue and gold, quasi-military uniform he's wearing, conducts eight or ten guys who also wear ill-fitting uniforms. Jerry's coffin is on a small stand, an American flag covering everything except the dent in its side. A guy with a bugle is off to the left. Ruthie sits on a folding chair in the first row, right in front of the casket. She has a wad of tissues in her hand and continually dabs the tears falling from her eyes. Father Celcius from the Newman Center sits next to Ruthie and does his best to console her. Talk about a thankless, can't win task.

The trip is taking forever. We're moving at about one mile an hour. We could get off the bus and walk to the stadium faster. Luckily, we have plenty of time. The game doesn't start until three.

We make the turn. We're on campus, going north toward the stadium, inching along past the old basketball arena. At the end of the cemetery, a section of the street has been blocked off, and where cars usually park, an old Army jeep sits. Steve Carlton, in

ROTC camouflage garb, stands on the Jeep's back seat like Douglas McArthur. I have to chuckle watching him order his ROTC cadets to line up in formation. The cadets don't want to be there. A number of them wave and scream, "Whack those Woodchucks!"

The players on the bus are pretty amazed at all of the hoopla going on. They look left, look right, stand up, change places, point out hot women, and make jokes. It's all a game before the game to them, but it's something more. I can feel it. It's all these different groups of people who don't belong together.

If you were to line up all the uniforms, none would come close to matching. In some way, the seas of people remind me of one of these power drinks that are becoming popular with athletes. You crack raw eggs, peel fruit, cut vegetables, spoon in gross stuff like wheat germ and soy powder, add milk, and plop it all into a blender. Hit *Puree*, and grind it all up into what they call a protein shake. It tastes terrible, but it's supposed to give you exceptional energy. I hate it. The scene out here is kinda like a protein drink. A whole bunch of different bunches of different stuff thrown together, whether they like it or not, waiting to be blended into an energizing concoction.

I see Cindy in the line-up of rooters to the right. She's with her sorority sisters, most of which are fat. They scream and wave like the rest of the Pioneer supporters. I don't see my frat brothers. They're probably busy stuffing cans of beer into their pockets before joining in the festivities.

In the front of the bus, Praytel is telling the driver to "get his ass in gear." The driver can't do anything; he's stuck. Why we ever took this route, beats the hell out of me.

Up to this point, it's all still fun. The band kicks into the Pioneer fight song for the millionth time this season; maybe it's the only song they know how to play. Behind the bus, and behind the band, a horde of people follow in cars, on foot, and on bikes; some pull wagons or push strollers. Many carry small American flags. Some carry *Stop the War* posters. Women pass out flowers.

Friends wave hello to acquaintances. The good news is no one seems to be bothering anyone else. The mood seems free, festive, and full of good expectation.

The bus travels another fifty yards and everything changes. Reaching the student union, we see ominous signs. Police, dressed in riot gear with Billy clubs in hand, are lined up on the outdoor stage like toy soldiers. They wear protective masks over their faces, padding on their chests, and gas masks dangle from their service belts. On the student union roof, between the two forty-foot banners of me, Police Chief Hurlbutt, Mayor Denton, and University President Schwartz lean over the railing watching the spectacle. Massive sound speakers are to their left, and behind them is a large bulletin board displaying a map of the campus. They aren't up there for the view. They're manning a command center.

A few feet from the intersection, down 13th Street, I see a wall of people approaching. They stretch at least twenty in width and a thousand in depth. Across the first row, held up by Marcus, Katie, and Molly, among others, is a banner four feet high and fifteen feet across with the words *Out Of Vietnam NOW*. Behind the banner, every imaginable type of human being follows: adults, kids, hippies, seniors, and all are clamoring to be heard. Some chant. Others pound drums. A few scream. Many sing. It's a cacophony of unrelated noise, all in the name of peace. Their sounds clash with the band playing and replaying the fight song; not one I would have requested for this scene.

Praytel is wailing at the driver to get the bus past the intersection before the crowd caves in on it, but the driver is stuck with nowhere to go. Inside the bus, the frivolity is replaced by a coming notion of fear, and with good reason, because behind the peace marchers are National Guardsmen in formation, guns at the ready, moving in step with the crowd. Once the crowd reaches the student union, they will be trapped between the Guardsmen in the street and the policemen on the stage.

Sitting high in the bus, I can see it all. It ain't pretty.

169

In seconds, the bus is engulfed in humanity. The marchers, football fans, on-lookers, ROTC cadets, Cindy and her sorority sisters, cheerleaders, band members, the curious, the confused, and the people, who just happen to be in the wrong place at the worst possible time, all converge in front of the student union like floodwaters reaching a delta.

Marcus, carrying a bullhorn in his hand, breaks off from his group and makes his way to the outdoor stage. Bravely, he stands in front of the row of armed cops, and announces, "We come in peace."

The marchers cheer.

"All we are saying is give peace a chance."

The crowd cheers, volume increasing.

Marcus continues. "No parent wants to lose a child, no wife wants to lose a husband, and no sibling wants to lose a brother or sister. Our leaders have to realize there is no point in losing another life in Vietnam. It is an unjust war, which has gone on too long, and its end is long past due." Marcus waits for the applause to cease before continuing. "We come together today to show solidarity in the cause, to have our voices heard, and to make the statement: We have had enough of the war in Vietnam, and we want out."

The loudest ovation of the day echoes across campus.

I watch Hurlbutt, Denton, and Schwartz peer down on Marcus—who has real guts to stand up there and speak, not a lot of brains, but a hell of a set of balls. The riot squad stands at the ready behind Marcus, but doesn't move. The National Guard stops their advance, and spreads out in a single line at the back of the demonstration with guns held chest high. Steve and his ROTC Cadets form a crooked line across University Avenue. The cheerleaders, band, and football aficionados don't really know what to do. They've been upstaged for something much more important than a football game, and they realize it. Our fans stand quietly waiting for it to be once again their turn.

"Join with me in song." Marcus urges the crowd, and begins

to sing, "How many roads must a man walk down, before they call him a man?  How many seas must a white dove sail, before she sleeps in the sand?"

I open the window of the bus, stick my head out to better see and hear. It is hard to believe, but calm suddenly exists. The marchers gently sway as they sing along with Marcus. I see Molly and Katie holding hands in front of the banner. The Guardsmen rest guns to their sides. The band members put instruments aside and join in singing with the marchers. The ROTC cadets are silent, as are the riot police. Families embrace. Strangers join hands. Couples hug. Players stand quietly showing reverence.

I look up on the roof and see only Schwartz remains on the railing. Hurlbutt and Denton are nowhere to be seen. In the distance I hear the faint rumblings of motorcycle engines and notes from a bugle.

"The answer is blowin' in the wind."

Quiet, absolute quiet, in the crowd.

"I ask all of you to raise your hands high and give the sign of peace in a gesture of love and friendship for all humanity," Marcus speaks.

Hands are raised and peace signs flashed to the sky. The entire assemblage stands still.

Marcus sings, "All we are saying is give peace a chance."

The crowd joins in. "All we are saying is give peace a chance."

And the loudspeakers erupt. "Your illegal assembly is now over. You are to disperse immediately." It's Hurlbutt at the microphone. "You've had your say; now go home."

Two riot cops come forward and relieve Marcus of his bullhorn. Marcus keeps his peace sign raised and sings the song as he is escorted off the stage and down a short flight of steps. "All we are saying is give peace a chance."

"You are ordered to disperse," explodes out of the speakers.

"All we are saying..."

"Now."

The song ends.

There are grumblings in the crowd, but no shouts of disappointment or anger. It is as if the marchers understand what they have come to prove has been accomplished, and they're now satisfied. All the different uniforms, ages, colors, and ethnic groups are not sure what to do next. They all stand, as if waiting for the other to make the first move. It's quiet, peaceful, and serene.

And gunshots ring out.

Loud, forceful, rifle shots disrupt the quiet vacuum like an air horn blasted at a basketball game.

The first volley stuns the crowd. The second causes heads to spin. The third, fourth, and fifth sends the crowd into a panic.

And the shots keep coming.

Parents grab their children. People scatter, fall to the ground, or scramble beneath any type of shelter or structure. Fear filled eyes search each and every way, but can't decipher the direction of the attack. Some are so scared they run in circles. Screams resound from every section of the crowd. Many scamper for the safety of school buildings, but find the doors locked.

Praytel is the first on the bus to dive under the seat; most others follow suit. The shots continue. Above the fray, I hang my head outside the bus and look back from where we came. At the edge of the cemetery, a line of uniformed men, stand with rifles raised, and shoot into the sky as directed by Diamond Jim.

Like gasoline being poured on a fire, the riot explodes. Marchers crash into each other attempting to flee. Women shout. Babies cry. Children hold onto parents for dear life. Our bus rocks from so many people outside banging on it in their attempt to find safety. Trash flies everywhere. What may have been precious once, has been dropped or left behind. Nothing matters except the safety of yourself and your loved ones.

The gunshots cease, but their damage has already been done.

"Move in," is heard from the loudspeakers. "Move in, now!"

Marchers run back down 13th street, see the National Guard advancing with rifles in hand, turn and run the other way. They collide into others, like offensive and defensive linemen when the ball is snapped. People are knocked to the ground. Some fall. Some trip. Some trample others. Nobody knows which way to turn. There's not a face in the crowd without panic etched upon it. Frightened folk rush to the safety of the student union, but find those doors also locked up tight. The band abandons their instruments and scatters like roaches from the nest. The rumble of motorcycle engines intensifies, as fifty black-leather-clad riders race their bikes into the center of the melee, causing more confusion and horror. A panicked few in the street pound on the door to the bus. Praytel screams at the driver, "Don't let them in. Whatever you do, don't let them in."

The cops come off the stage with clubs raised, and push the crowd back into the street. If they run into someone attempting to break through their line, they have no hesitation in using their Billy clubs. For the first time, I see blood.

I'm the only one standing on the bus. The others have either ducked under the seats or lie on top. I go up and down the aisle, looking left, right, forward, and back. I can't believe what I see. Fights are breaking out, heads are getting bashed, voices scream blame, and fists fly. The motorcycle gang literally mows down anyone in their errant paths. The ROTC cadets aren't sure what to do, even though Steve stands on the jeep barking out orders. I get to the back of the bus, and see Diamond Jim leading the charge of his rifle-toting, honor guard buddies into the fray like their storming the beach on D-Day. But half-way down the block, Diamond Jim stops, grabs his chest, and falls to the ground. I watch as he gasps for breath.

The loudspeakers continue a diatribe of, "Disperse, disperse immediately or you will be arrested." Hurlbutt is making the chaotic situation worse with every word he bellows.

Bottles, cans, and trash are flying through the air. The grounds are littered with everything from posters, to strollers, to banners, to roses.

I search the chaos for Marcus, Molly, and Katie, anyone I

know, but find no one. And that's when I see the first canister sail into the fray. When it hits the pavement, it doesn't explode, but spews out a white smoke, which hangs in the air like a thick fog. One whiff of tear gas and your eyes water, your lungs ache, and you become disoriented. I look up to the roof of the student union and see other canisters being launched into the crowd. I hear the sound of choking, and wails of pain from burning eyes. The only ones who don't suffer from the canister's effects are the cops and guardsmen, who immediately don their gas masks, which make them pig-like in appearance. Now I know where the term originated.

Guys scream for me to close the window of the bus, and as I do so, I see an older black man on his knees, leaning over Diamond Jim, administering mouth-to-mouth resuscitation. For some reason, I head for the front of the bus where the view out of the big windshield is better. A hand comes out of the floor and grabs my ankle. I can't proceed. I look down. The hand belongs to Lester Tollinger, who is lying beneath a seat. Terror is on his face; tears are in his eyes. "Make it stop," he begs. "Make them stop, Tony."

"I'll try," I assure the overgrown coward, and he releases his grasp.

Moving forward, I see Marcus run past the front of the bus, up the stairs of the student union stage, and leap onto the top of the canopy of the building. He takes hold, lifting himself up, and crawls upward to the cement ledge of the building.

Hurlbutt's voice bellows into the PA system, "Stop, or you will be arrested."

With each word, the riot goes one more mile-per-hour into overdrive.

Marcus moves down the ledge, balancing himself until he reaches the corner, where he strains to reach up and grab two wires plugged into the electrical box outlet.

"Leave this campus now. I order you to leave this campus..."

Marcus pulls the plug. Hurlbutt's voice goes silent.

174

I can't hear, but I can read the word on Hurlbutt's lips as he peers over to see Marcus on the ledge below. The word I recognize is "Nigger."

With the PA system out, I hear the chant, "Hell no, we won't go. Hell no, we won't go." It comes from the opposite end of the student union building. I can't decipher how many voices, but it's a lot.

For a fleeting second I see someone I recognize, Father Celcius. He's running across the street, heading for I don't know what, and a biker on a Harley runs him down like a dog. The priest is down, squirming on the ground, holding his left knee. He struggles to get to his feet, but is hit again; this time by a teenager who is so scared he seems to be running from himself. I think about going out to help, but at that instant, the first flame flies through the air. It's clear, round, a bottle with a rag sticking out its spout. The cloth is on fire. I watch the firebomb fly over the union's front steps, past the picture windows, and burst into a pool of liquid fire at the edge of the outdoor stage. The Touchdown Tony banner is first to catch fire and the forty-foot Passing Pioneer lights up the afternoon sky. The second flaming projectile soon arrives, this one landing in the street, scattering the rioters and police.

"Hell no, we won't go. Hell no, we won't go." Hayden is leading the chorus, as his henchmen behind him launch two more Molotov cocktails into the riot arena. If it is possible for the people to get any more panicked, these fireballs do the trick. One firebomb hits near the bus and scatters the people trying to climb aboard. The second hits an abandoned stroller left on the sidewalk and bursts into flames. The noise, smoke, and fire all add to the chaotic confusion. This is absolute madness.

The National Guard breaks formation, which allows a passageway up University. It doesn't take long for many in the crowd to find this escape route. The ROTC offers no resistance, much to Steve's dismay. A number of the guardsmen join the escapees running north, much to the consternation of General

August Brown, who, like Steve, has lost control of his troops. Brown resembles a sprung jack-in-the box, as he jumps, waves, and jives in an attempt to stop the retreat of his own men. What an asshole.

Hurlbutt's riot police have no intention of leaving the scene. They indiscriminately swing their clubs at whoever may be in striking distance. They're enjoying their work. One cop on the stage runs around the flames, takes aim with a spent, tear gas canister, and throws it like a baseball, aiming at Marcus who's crouched down on the student union ledge. It's a strike, hitting Marcus on the left side of his head. Marcus' knees buckle, he crumbles, and falls off the ledge landing on the hard concrete of the stage. The policeman wastes no time clubbing my unprotected and wounded tutor.

I run down the two steps, grab the door handle to the bus and pull. It won't open. "Open the damn door," I scream at the driver who is on the floor, cowering in the fetal position.

"Now!"

"No." I hear from the first row.

The cop continues to beat Marcus with his club. "Open the damn door," I repeat.

"Those bastards aren't getting in here," Praytel screams back at me.

I come up the stairs, and repeat for the third time, "Open the damn door."

Praytel gets in my face. "You shut up, and do what you're told."

I reach out with two hands, grab my coach by the throat, lift him off the ground, and propel him through the air six rows down the aisle. He falls on his back like a tackling dummy in Spring Training. With Praytel down and not getting up, I grab the driver, pick him off the floor, and order, "Open the door. Now!"

The little man hits an air release switch, the door opens, and I run out. One second after I'm out, the door closes.

The tear gas burns. There's fire at my feet. I run across the street, step over people cowering around a cement bench. I fight my way through the trash and up onto the stage. I sprint as if I'm running for yardage daylight, and tackle the cop beating on Marcus. He tries to get up, but I grab him again and with one hand on the back of his belt and one hand on the back of his shirt collar, I throw him head first into the plate glass window. He doesn't get up.

Marcus is unconscious, bleeding from his forehead. I get him up, onto my shoulder, and carry him off the stage. I'm heading for the bus, but a tear gas canister hits me square in my left kidney. I go down. Marcus sprawls helplessly on the ground. The white smoke is belching out of the gas can. I can barely focus, but get to my feet. I limp over to the smoking can, burn my hand picking it up, turn, and see Denton leaning over the railing staring right at me. I cock my arm and throw a perfect spiral, hitting the mayor right on his fat head. He goes down amid the thick, white smoke from the canister.

I put my ugly tie to my mouth, so I can breathe, pick Marcus back up and onto my back, and run as fast as I've ever run to the door of the bus. I pound until the driver opens, and load Marcus inside. "Get to a hospital, now!"

I push his body as far onto the bus as I can, but have to go back outside to get his feet inside. I look up and see Arthur help lift Marcus further onto the bus. "He's hurt. Get him to a hospital."

"I will," Arthur assures me.

Outside, I see a woman with a small, frightened child. I run to her, wrap my arms around her, and carry her to the bus door. It opens again and she climbs inside. Three or four others follow and are pulled up into the bus by my halfback.

A fight breaks out ten feet from me. Ralph, Ernie, and Sean are slugging it out with four of the America First members; must have been lousy beer. I find Father Celcius crouched in the corner, gripping his leg, wincing in pain. "Father…"

"I can't move."

177

I put his arm over my neck, and the two of us hobble back to the bus, which is actually starting to move. We do our best to run alongside. Arthur must see me from the inside because the bus stops, the door opens, and I hand the priest over to Arthur. The door again closes.

One step to my left, I meet Molly face-to-face. She carries a high school girl whose eyes have completely glazed over. She must be in shock.

"There're people hurt over there," Molly tells me pointing in the direction of the athletic offices. She runs off, as I get the girl onto the bus, and into Arthur's waiting arms. "Now go," I order and the bus begins to move.

I run, following Molly, but I lose her almost immediately.

I hear, "Hell no, we won't go." I smell the lingering tear gas. I feel the heat of the burning liquid. Cops wreak havoc on anyone who looked as if they were protesting. I pull one cop away from a helpless kid and feel a shot to my ribs. I go down, but before the next blow hits, I roll over, kick upward, and my foot lands in the crotch of the policeman; the one place on his body he failed to protect. I get up and scamper away. I find myself twenty or so feet from the ROTC Jeep and see Molly. She is nose to nose with Steve, who carries a weeping Cindy in his arms. I can't hear what Molly says, but Steve's words are clear: "Fucking bitch."

Steve drops Cindy, straightens up, and slaps Molly across her face. He catches her before she goes down and locks his hands around her throat.

"Don't," I scream.

"This is all her fault," Steve yells back at me.

"Let her go."

Steve's grip tightens. Molly's eyes bulge, as she gasps for air. She tries to slap her way out of the hold, but with no air, she has no strength. I run forward, fist cocked, and hit Steve so hard I feel the bones in his jaw crack beneath my knuckles.

Steve goes down on his back, out cold. For some reason, I will never understand, I stand over him and say, "Don't you get it?

178

They're right."

Cindy jumps on my back, her arms flailing like a third grader in a schoolyard fight. I toss her off like lint. On the ground, she curls up in a ball and weeps.

Molly is pushed up against the side of the Jeep, gasping for air. She looks up at me and says, "I haven't been hit that hard since my step-daddy."

I lift her up off the ground, and hold her in my arms. "I'm sorry, Molly. I am so, so sorry."

Amidst the terror, destruction, tear gas, and flames, we embrace as if long lost lovers finally reunited.

And it hits me. A Billy club to the back of my neck, hitting harder than any blindsiding linebacker has ever hit me. I go down. I'm hit again. I try to get up, but all I can manage to do is scream at Molly, "Run."

I'm hit again, and again, and again. I cover my head, but it provides little protection. The blows come fast and furious. I can't see, but there must be three or four guys bringing down the havoc. I'm pretty much out of it and a bloody mess. I'm flipped over onto my stomach, my arms are bent behind me, and cuffs snapped onto my wrists.

The next thing I know, I'm on the floor of a paddy wagon, surrounded by a lot of people in a lot worse shape than me.

"Hey," one says. "Aren't you Touchdown Tony?"

## CHAPTER 23

I'm crammed into a holding cell, designed for maybe four, but now holding at least thirty. Nobody inside can move. Every muscle in my body aches; I wonder what's broken. There are only men in my cell, but across the room is another holding tank filled with women. My head is spinning, worse than any morning hangover. I must lose consciousness and fall at some point, because I remember waking up crumbled into a ball on the floor. Other inmates try to help me, but there is not a hell of a lot they can do.

I have no idea how long I'm in the cell, but after I pass in and out of consciousness a third or fourth time, the number inside the cell has lessened. There is now room to move, but I can't. Pain shoots through me like red-hot needles if I try to move even an inch. I lie down across the front of the cell and try to be still. At the end of the hall, past the women's holding cell, the big hand on the clock reaches twelve and the little hand is on the three. Game time.

Every few minutes a voice in the hallway announces a name, and someone inside answers, "Here." Keys come out, and the door of the cell slides open. The "Here" person exits and is escorted down the hallway by two uniformed guards. A few minutes go by, and the scene repeats. In one instance, I see a man in a suit being led to the women's holding cell. I watch him stand at the door, point inside, and tell the guard, "That's her."

A few seconds later, I watch Katie go down the hallway, the guard on one arm, her father on the other. "Wait 'til I get you home," are the only words spoken.

One last time, I pass out, fall asleep, black out, whatever you want to call it. When I awaken, the clock at the end of the hall reads six o'clock. Morning or night, I wonder. My mouth is dry, my head a bit clearer, the pain remains in every cell of my body, but the intensity has diminished. I can move, but not very quickly. On the side of my head, my hair is matted in dried blood. I have massive black and blue bruises on my arms and legs. The skin on my throwing hand is crusty from the burn. My eyesight is blurry. I can't seem to focus near or far. My urine is red, not yellow. On what's left of my green sports jacket, you can barely make out the green. The bloodstains have dried into a rust color; the dirt and the grime is either black or dark gray. The coat is torn in too many places to mention. My tan slacks, if you can imagine, are in worse shape. My Pioneer *Go to the game* uniform won't even make a good cleaning rag.

I'm alone in the holding cell. I'm the last leaf on the criminal tree—lucky me.

An hour later, two guards come down the hall. There's no point in calling out my name, and they don't. They unlock the cell and enter.

"Get up."

I slowly rise.

One guard turns me around, and the other shackles my hands behind my back. Both lead me out of the cell and down the hallway. I don't bother asking any questions because these two don't seem the type to answer. Reaching the end of the hallway we turn right instead of left, unlike the others I saw leaving the cell. We pass through a metal security door into what first resembles a small locker room, but with no lockers. There are cement floors, toilet stalls along one wall, and urinals along another. At the back of the room are two tiled stalls, one has a shower and one doesn't. The guard, who cuffed me in the cell, uncuffs me. "Get undressed."

I do as I'm told.

"Now stand over there." The second guard points to the stall with no showerhead coming out of the wall.

I walk into the enclosed area, and as I do, the first guard picks up a garden hose, adjusts the nozzle, and very cold water sprays my naked body. I jump around shivering at first, but the water does begin to warm.

"There's soap over there."

I take my time washing myself, especially the dried blood out of my scalp. I can feel where I've been cut. My body is a mass of bruises, some already discolored, many more soon to follow suit. With every move, I'm more positive I've got a couple of broken ribs. My neck is especially painful where I took the first blindside blow. Just as the water gets nice and warm, the hose is turned off, a towel is thrown to me, and I'm told, "Dry off."

"Come on."

Wrapped in the wet towel, I'm led to an anteroom and told to sit on the gurney table. I obey. A few minutes later a nurse comes into the room. "You're Touchdown Tony, right?"

"I used to be."

She begins to examine me, paying particular attention to the gash on my head, and the burn mark on my hand.

"Who won the game?" I ask her.

"You don't know?"

"No."

She gives me a smirk. "Woodchucks."

"What was the score?"

"I think they called it two to nothing."

My hearing must be off, too. "Two-zip?"

She smoothes a white medicine onto my scalp, and says, "They said when one team forfeits, the score becomes two to zero."

"I didn't know that," I tell her.

"Neither did most of the people in the stands when they announced it."

She applies some salve to my hand, tells me the only bones broken seem to be my ribs, and there's not much you can do for broken ribs. "Good luck," she tells me as she leaves.

I'm given an orange, one-piece jail suit to wear. I put it on, but it doesn't fit, too small. I wonder if the uniforms in my life will ever end. I tend to doubt it.

The guards re-shackle my hands, and we walk out of the anteroom, through the bathroom/locker room, down the hall, and

I'm deposited into my own cell. I lie down on the bed that's six inches too short, and fall asleep.

---

"McIntyre."

The loud, booming voice wakes me up.

"You got a visitor."

The first move from horizontal to vertical is a killer.

The guard unlocks the door and comes into the cell. He takes me by the arm to stand me up. "You going to be a good boy?" He asks.

"Yeah, I promise."

He leads me by the arm out of the cell. We walk down the aisle, past fellow inmates. Not a lot of college kids, as I would have expected; it's mostly drunks. One asks, "Are you really Touchdown Tony?"

The guard leads me into a small, square, windowless room. On one wall there is a large glass mirror. In the middle of the room is a table with two chairs on one side, and one on the other. "Sit there," he says and points to the one chair.

Once I'm seated, I see him nod his head.

A door on the opposite side of the room opens.

"Mom."

She rushes forward, but is stopped before reaching me.

"No touching," the guard informs her. "Sit."

My mother sits across from me. "Are you okay?"

"They said I had some broken ribs."

She sees my hand. "Your throwing hand got burned?"

"It's okay."

She looks up at the matted hair on my head. "You got cut?"

"A couple times."

"What the hell got into you?" she asks.

"I don't know," I say. "Maybe truth, justice, and the American way."

183

"This is no time to be funny."

"I'm not being funny."

"Everybody else is out on bail," she tells me, "but they set yours at half a million dollars."

"Why?"

"No Rose Bowl."

"Seems a bit much, doesn't it?"

"They're making an example out of you. They want to set the price for any long-haired hippie freak who wants to physically protest authority in this town."

"I'm a trendsetter."

"Justice is finding us a lawyer. We're going to fight this Tony. We have way too much riding on you to see it all crumble into nothing." She stops, but starts right back in again, "How could you, Tony? How could you?"

"How could I what?"

"Put yourself in the middle of a riot?"

"The police were beating the crap out people."

"And that became your problem?"

"It was a gang of thugs going after people who didn't have a chance."

"And you thought you, alone, all by yourself, could stop a riot?"

"I wasn't thinking..."

Mom cuts me off, "Obviously."

"I was reacting."

"To what?"

"To what the hell was going on."

"It was a riot!"

"It was a peaceful protest until these idiots starting shooting, and all hell breaks loose."

She leans close to me. "What the hell do you know about protests?"

"I think those people in the street were right."

"Right?"

184

"Yes."

She screams into my face, "Tony, stop thinking. Would you just stop thinking?"

"I can't."

"Yes, you can."

"Mom..."

"No one cares what you think, Tony. What you think doesn't make any difference. The only thing that matters is to get your ass out of here and back on the field."

My head starts to spin. This is all way too much to comprehend.

Her voice remains at a fevered pitch. "Don't say anything to anybody. Keep your mouth shut. If someone asks you a question, don't answer. Don't get into a conversation with anyone. Don't admit anything. If you have to say something, say, 'I'm not guilty.' And keep saying it until they shut up." She hesitates, "Can you do that?"

My head falls into my hands. The spinning won't stop.

"I'm going to try to get you out of here, but if I can't, I can't."

I can't answer. I squeeze my head to make it stop, but the spinning only gets worse.

"Justice is getting the best attorney money can buy."

"Great," I manage to say without the proper enthusiasm.

"He told me to tell you it's going to be okay."

"Great."

"I'm sure they're going to speed the arraignment up, while the case is still front page news," she says. "So, it's important you keep your mouth shut."

I lift my head as best as I'm able. I peer out with unfocused eyes at my mother. "How's Dad?"

"He's the same, Tony," she snaps back at me. "If I were you, I wouldn't be worrying about Daddy, I'd be worrying about myself."

"I think we've had enough," the guard says. He comes forward and takes me by the arm.

"We're going to get you out of this, Tony," Mom assures me.

"If they try to question you, tell them you won't answer without a lawyer present." She pauses as I am led to the door. "And don't do anything stupid while you're in here."

Before I'm out the door, I turn and say to Mom, "Thanks for stopping by."

The guard leads me back down the hall. I stumble a few times on the way. He gets me into my cell, takes the cuffs off, and sits me down, so I don't fall.

I lie down on the bed. I hear the door clang shut, and the guard walking back down the hall. I rest my head on my laced fingers, and stare upward at the black, cement ceiling. For some reason, I don't attempt to understand that it feels good to be alone.

## CHAPTER 24

The dizzy spells end the next day. My eyesight is no longer blurred. I can feel a large scab on the top of my head, but the area is still very painful to touch. My ribs still hurt, but the rest of my body is recuperating. The color of the bruises is starting to fade.

The food is terrible. The cell is cold and damp. I ask for an extra blanket, but my request is answered with a laugh. I didn't consider it a joke. My urine has gone from red to pink. I lose all track of time. I spend most of the hours on my back staring at the ceiling. I wonder what happened to Marcus. He was bleeding and unconscious the last time I saw him. I wonder what happened to Molly; did she get away? I could care less about Steve and Cindy, but wonder if Diamond Jim died.

I think very little about myself. I've never been in jail, never dreamed of being in jail, and now I'm in jail. I don't know what to think.

I've been here two days, or maybe three; I'm not sure. I haven't left the cell. No one comes to visit. No one comes to question me, talk to me, or trick me into confessing to whatever I'm supposed to confess to. Maybe all those scenes you see on TV, where the cops beat a confession out of the perpetrator, are made up. The only people I see are guards and the nurse who stops by to give me a follow up examination. "You bounce back pretty quickly," she tells me.

---

The clang of a club against the bars awakens me.

"Rise and shine, Touchdown Tony," the guard orders.

I remain in second gear when I rise. My muscles ache when I am forced to move at any speed faster than *slow*.

"Come on," he says. "I don't got all day."

We return to the no-locker, locker room.

Of all the guards I've had the pleasure of meeting during my stay, this one is the biggest jerk. When he cuffs me, he makes sure he twists my arms to elicit plenty of pain, he doesn't lead me down the hall, he pushes me, and he thoroughly enjoys watching me shower. "That guy you kicked in the balls is a good friend of mine," he told me yesterday.

After my shower, I am directed to a sink, where a razor, shaving cream, toothpaste, and brush sit on the shelf. "Make yourself pretty, pretty boy," he tells me.

The blade in the razor is a relic. It's difficult removing almost a week's worth of stubble. I nick myself a number of times. I'm given a clean orange suit, underwear, and socks. My wrists are shackled behind my back after a rough twist of each arm. I am led back to the square meeting room, where the handcuffs are removed. I'm told to sit in the same chair as before.

A few minutes later my mom, and a man I've never met, enter.

"How are you?"

"Better."

"This is Dustin Gaylord," Mom says. "He'll be representing you."

The man is short, maybe five-six, and has a few wisps of hair left on his head. He's probably around fifty, but looks sixty. The only things shinier than his suit and two diamond rings are his shoes.

"I'm sorry we couldn't meet sooner. I flew in last night."

I nod my head. What else am I going to do?

"You know how this works?"

I shake my head at the man. "No."

"This morning is your arraignment. You will stand before the judge and the charges against you will be announced. You are not to say a word. The judge may or may not ask the prosecutors to reveal the evidence supporting the charges. No witnesses will be called, but the victims will be in the courtroom, and in clear view of the bench. Again, keep your mouth shut. I will then ask the

188

judge for all charges against you to be dismissed. I will explain you were acting in self-defense, and got caught up in a riot you had nothing to do with. I've made sure there will be a number of people in the courtroom on your side. They'll be ready to make some noise"

I interrupt, "What are their names?"

"I don't remember."

"One of them Molly?"

"He doesn't remember," Mom says.

"The prosecutor will undoubtedly have the police chief and mayor front and center. I'm sure he'll try to throw in some bullshit about you being a violent hothead who was out to destroy society as we know it." Gaylord pauses. "No matter what happens, what comments are made, what anyone screams out in the courtroom, don't say a word."

I look down at the little man. I don't like him.

"The charges against you will be read. At this point, the judge may ask you for a statement. If he does, just shake your head *no*."

"Maybe I should say something," I say.

"What?" My mom shouts out.

"That I shouldn't be the one on trial here. It was the cops who were wrong and that asshole police chief who thought he'd be Hitler for the afternoon."

"Don't. You can only hurt yourself," Gaylord says.

"But it's the truth," I raise my voice.

"Are you out of your mind, Tony?" Mother yells.

"It's the right thing to do."

"This is a court of law," Gaylord says. "Right and wrong have nothing to do with it."

"But..."

"Wake up, Tony," mom continues. "He's here to get your ass out of here. Do what he says."

I look at my mother. She suddenly reminds me of all the coaches I've had in the past who believed berating me would motivate me.

189

"People should know the truth," I say.

"Well, it's not for you to tell them," Mom says.

"If I don't tell them, who will?" I ask.

"Who cares?"

"Your life is at stake here, Tony," Gaylord says. "Leave it to me. I know how the system works. I'll make mincemeat out of these backwoods lawyers."

"Tony," Mother says, "we know what's best. Do as you're told and you'll be back on your way to being the next Joe Namath."

"Is that all you want me to be, Mom?"

"That's enough for anyone to be."

I sit without moving for a moment. Then I nod my head, as if to say, "I got it."

There are a few seconds of silence before Gaylord continues. "Next, the judge will ask 'Mr. McIntyre, how do you plead?'"

"And you say," Mother adds, "not guilty."

"The judge will set dates for the preliminaries, and that will be it." Gaylord takes a breath, backs up one step, and says, "I'll do what I can to get your bail reduced, but don't hold out a lot of hope. The rednecks in this cow town are out for your blood, Tony."

"Lucky me."

"Do you understand?" Mom asks. "All you say is 'not guilty.'"

"Yeah. Pretty simple game plan."

"I'll have you back on the field throwing touchdowns in a month, trust me," Gaylord assures me.

---

The courthouse is four blocks from the jail. Besides the iron on my wrists, my favorite guard adds a pair of leg shackles that really cut into the skin above my ankles. Gaylord argues this is unnecessary, cruel, and unusual punishment, but the guard doesn't listen. My attorney loses his first argument.

It is a cold, dreary, rainy day, fitting for my situation.

I'm loaded into the back of a squad car, seated between Gaylord and Mom. An additional patrol car provides escort for the five-minute drive. I guess you can never be too careful.

"What the hell are you doing?" Gaylord screams as the cop pulls up to the front steps of the courthouse. "Even in this town, you got to have a rear entrance."

The cop driving doesn't respond. He gets out, opens the back door and orders us out of the car. Two cops from the escort car come to walk us inside. I need the help, because there is a gaggle of news reporters, cameras, and microphones aimed at me the second my head is out the door. Ace Dunnigan is at the head of the pack, wouldn't you know it.

The reporters beg for a statement and scream out questions. I follow the plan, and don't say a word. I hobble up the steps; it's very difficult to walk with chains dangling from both hands and feet.

Inside the courthouse, it's worse. The place is packed, at least three deep on each side of the hallway, a gauntlet of gawkers. I keep my head down. I hear insults, praise, anger, and one "Way to go, Tony." The three cops, Gaylord, Mom, and I enter an unmarked door, and find ourselves in a small room. I am handed over to another guy in a uniform different from ones the police wear. The badge on his arm reads: *Bailiff*.

"We will see you in the courtroom," Gaylord tells me, as he, Mom, and the cops exit the room.

I'm not sure what to do. I watch the bailiff watching me. "Nice day for a hanging, uh?" I say to break the tension.

"We'll see," he says.

I lean against the wall to rest. I'm exhausted. I would rather be in my cell taking a nap, but thoughts crowd into my brain like students rushing for fifty-yard line seats. I think of my mom, my dad, my life, but from different angles. They appear distorted and foreign in ways I've never imagined. One image of my mother stands out from all others. She's standing over me, encapsulating me like a dark cloud smothering my senses. I can't speak, see, or hear. I panic, try to think, but I'm helpless. A chill runs up and down my spine.

A knock comes on the door.

"Showtime," the bailiff says. He takes me by the wrists and escorts me out of the room.

The courtroom is wall-to-wall bodies. So many it is hard to make out the faces, but one I clearly see. She's in the back and must be standing on a chair. I see her lips move. Molly's telling me, 'they wouldn't let me see you.' I give her a wink and a smile.

I am led into the room to the table on the right where Gaylord waits. Behind him in the first row is my Mom, Dad in his wheelchair, and Justice Segalman. Dad doesn't look good. I feel horrible he has to witness this. At the table to the left are two men in nice suits. Behind them in the first row are Chief Hurlbutt, Mayor Denton, who sports a bandage across one side of his head, and Praytel; it's obvious whose side he's playing for now. I see Arthur; he folds his hands and whispers what I hope is a prayer. A few others in the room, I slightly recognize.

Gaylord turns me around quickly as the bailiff announces, "All rise."

The judge is tall, younger than I would have guessed, maybe forty, and athletic. I'll bet he played basketball in his younger years. "Be seated."

The bailiff reads off a clipboard, "The State versus Anthony Michael McIntyre. The Honorable Judge Joseph T. Haggerty presiding."

I sit.

"Mr. McIntyre."

"Yes, sir," I answer Judge Haggerty, much to the consternation of Gaylord.

"It is 'yes, Your Honor'," the judge corrects me.

"Yes, Your Honor."

"Stand up."

I rise.

"Is all the hardware necessary?" the judge asks. "This is a first offense, is it not?"

Gaylord glares over to the opposition's table with an "*I told you so*" stare.

"Due to the severity, and the nature of the attacks upon people currently in this room, it was determined safety be a priority durlng these proceedings."

"Safety is one thing, Mr. Truss, but parading the accused as if he's Jack the Ripper, is quite another. Remove the restraints."

The cop, who drove us to the courthouse, comes forward and frees me.

"Thank you, Judge, those things really hurt."

Gaylord nudges me as I make the comment.

"I wouldn't know," the judge says. "Bailiff, read the charges."

The bailiff steps forward, and reads from the first sheet on his clipboard. "One count of unlawful assembly, one count of refusal to disperse, one count of interfering with a police action, two counts of aggravated assault, and one count of assault with a deadly weapon."

Gaylord speaks up. "These charges are past ridiculous, Your Honor." Gaylord raises a few papers in his right hand, and waves them for all to see. "Motion to dismiss all charges."

Leonard Truss, the prosecutor, counters with, "We're not in agreement, Your Honor. If the Court is going to consider it, we would like to be heard."

"Counselors, please approach the bench."

Gaylord motions for me to sit as he and Truss move forward to the edge of the bench where Judge Haggerty sits above them. They talk, but I can't hear. In a few seconds, the two attorneys return to their respective tables.

"The motion is denied," Judge Haggerty is quick to rule.

That's two down for my attorney.

Gaylord lifts a second set of papers. "Motion to reduce all charges to misdemeanors."

Judge Haggerty leans forward towards Gaylord. "What did we just discuss?"

"Your Honor," Gaylord says. "This case is already a miscarriage of justice. My client, who has already been tried in the press, was merely a victim of circumstances."

Not to be outdone, Truss jumps into the verbal fray, "Judge, if you would like to read over the preliminary evidence report, it will clearly reveal, in detail, the multiple felonies attributed to Mr. McIntyre."

Gaylord again, "Judge, this is nothing more than a small town lynching. My client is being charged with the entire blame for a riot he had no involvement in planning, carrying out, or participating. In the courtroom there are eyewitnesses that can give sworn testimony that my client's actions were not only in self-defense, but for the benefit of people seriously injured in the melee. I am merely giving the court an opportunity to end this charade before it goes on any further."

"Judge," Truss interrupts, "you will not have to go far to hear from two victims of Mr. McIntyre's actions. Police Chief Hurlbutt and Mayor Denton will provide a minute-by-minute account of the vicious and unlawful action of Mr. McIntyre."

"I beg you, Judge," Gaylord says, "before this town, university, and your courtroom become laughingstocks of the nation for what you're doing to a Heisman Trophy candidate."

Judge Haggerty asks the attorneys, "Are you two finished?"

"I am if you put a stop to this idiocy," Gaylord answers.

"That was a yes or no question, Counselor."

Gaylord swallows his next words.

The crowd in the courtroom isn't sure what to do. It is as new to them, as it is new to me.

The judge hesitates for a moment, and speaks softly, "I would like to remind both counsel today's court proceeding is an arraignment. And there are no witnesses at an arraignment. You may save your witnesses, thoughts, theories, evidence, and hyperbole for the trial, if one is held." He looks at Mr. Gaylord. "You can file your motions with the clerk after this hearing if you are still inclined, Counselor, and a hearing will be set in due course. But for today's proceeding, there is only one question to be asked, and one to be answered. Do I make myself perfectly clear?"

Both lawyers respond, "Yes, Your Honor."

Judge Haggerty rests back in his chair. He peers down at me, looks me straight in the eye, paying no attention to anything or anyone else in the courtroom. "Mr. McIntyre, please stand."

I do as I'm told. Gaylord also rises.

Judge Haggerty clears his throat and speaks to me with a slight glint in his eye. "Tony, you were a pretty busy boy that Saturday."

I get another nudge, but shake my head in the affirmative.

"Do you realize there are some very serious charges leveled against you?"

I nod my head again.

"I'm sure your attorney has explained that two of these charges carry multiple years of incarceration, if you are convicted."

"I know."

Gaylord thumps me in my sore ribs. "He has, Your Honor."

Judge Haggerty continues, "If you choose to plead 'Not Guilty,' in all probability there will be a trial, and it will be months before a verdict is reached. You may be held in custody the entire time. The trial may be a long and painful process. But there is a lot at stake here, and this is your decision." The judge pauses. "Do you understand?"

I nod.

"Mr. McIntyre, I'm sure your attorney has advised you, and I expect you have thought long and hard about the question I am about to ask." The Judge pauses. The courtroom is deathly quiet.

I turn slightly to my left and see Molly. Tears are streaming down her face. I see Lester Tollinger, who has a total blank look on his face. Closer to me, Praytel has a snarl, Hurlbutt and Denton sport lines of hatred, and my mother is on an edge I've never seen her on before. Dad stares at me. I can't tell if he understands what's going on or not.

"To the charges against you, Anthony McIntyre, do you plead guilty or not guilty?"

I hesitate.

"Answer him," Gaylord tells me.

I feel my mother's presence behind me like a defensive lineman ready to throw me for a loss.

"Mr. McIntyre," the judge repeats. "How do you plead?"

"I'm not sure."

"Tony!" my Mom screams out.

There's a gasp from the crowd.

"Request permission to have a word with my client," Gaylord asks the judge.

"Denied." The judge asks me, "What aren't you sure about?"

"Tony, don't say anything. Just say 'Not guilty'," my mother screams from the front row.

The bailiff hurries over to restrain and quiet her.

I turn. My mother's eyes and mine meet. For a few seconds we stare into each others' souls. I see an opponent, not a teammate. "I'm calling my own plays now, Mom."

"Tony don't!"

I turn back to the court. "I'm supposed to tell the truth, aren't I, Judge?" I ask.

"That would be preferable."

"And if I go to trial, I have to tell the truth, or I'll get myself in more trouble than I'm already in; if that's even possible."

The judge smiles, "Yes."

"Tony, please," my mother begs.

Gaylord says to me, "Tony, shut up."

"I can't deny anything I did that day. I kicked that cop in the balls, I tossed my coach about nine rows on that bus, and I picked up a tear gas canister and tried to knock some sense into the idiot mayor we have in this town. If there had been another canister available, I would have thrown one at Hurlbutt, too. What I saw that day was horrible. The people who were in charge acted like

196

third grade bullies, but with a real army at their disposal. My friend Marcus, who was trying to stop the chaos, was attacked. When they had him down on the ground and helpless, the cops pummeled him with their Billy clubs like a bunch of thugs. I saw cops attack innocent protestors for no reason. I saw: women getting beaten, frightened kids, bloodied heads, people so scared they didn't know what to do. The protestors didn't start the riot; they were singing a song for peace when the whole place went bullshit. And they didn't escalate it either. The police chief and mayor can take the trophy for that event. The actions of the police, National Guard, Hurlbutt, and Denton were nothing less than cruel, hateful, and inhumane. You can read the list of charges against me over and over again, but all I can truthfully say, is I did only one thing wrong that day."

"And what was that, Tony?" the Judge asks.

"I didn't get my ass off the bus soon enough."

There is a collective gasp in the courtroom. And, for a few fleeting seconds, not a cell in my body or mind is in pain.

Judge Haggerty sits back in his chair, as if he needs time to take it all in.

I turn to see my mother slumped in the chair, her face buried in her hands. She's crying.

Gaylord says to me, "You stupid fool."

Molly has a smile on her face, as does Arthur.

Truss speaks up, "May I remind the court that Mr. McIntyre has not yet answered the question."

"Be that as it may, Mr. McIntyre," the judge says to me, "in the eyes of the law, guilt or innocence must be declared. How do you plead?"

"In my own eyes, and hopefully in the eyes of God, I'm innocent, but, I guess, in the eyes of the law, I'm about as guilty as you can get."

The courtroom explodes. People scream, shout, cheer, and cry. Evidently, no one expected this.

The gavel comes down.

Judge Haggerty speaks, "Bailiff, please set a date on the calendar for sentencing and return the accused to custody."

One more slap of the gavel and Judge Haggerty leaves the bench.

It's over.

My mother won't look at me. Gaylord is disgusted; he packs his papers into his briefcase without a word. I turn to my dad. He has the same look on his face as before. I'm still not sure what he's thinking. I get closer to him and he reaches up with his one good hand, and touches my arm. I lean over, my ear close to his mouth, and I hear him say, "You did good. I've never been so proud of my son."

## CHAPTER 25

I cut a deal.

Molly found me an ACLU lawyer, and it was wrapped up in a week. Three years with the possibility of an early parole, based on good behavior. I'd also get credit for time served.

I am going to prison. I'm a convicted felon, and will be for the remainder of my life. But, my sentence does provide a silver lining to the dark cloud. Felons are not eligible to serve in the armed forces. I'm out of the draft but at a very steep price.

Molly visited every day I was in jail. Arthur came, and to my surprise, Ralph and Ernie showed up to say hello. They said they had never been inside a jail, and wanted to see what it was like. I'm not sure they were impressed. They told me Steve had to have his jaw wired shut, and announcement time, after dinner at the frat house, had never been so much fun.

Molly told me Diamond Jim did suffer a heart attack when he and his boys went charging into the riot like Teddy Roosevelt and his Rough Riders. An older black man named Roy saw Diamond Jim go down, rushed to him, figured out the problem, and administered mouth to mouth. The ambulance arrived twenty minutes later, while Roy was still puffing away. The driver said, "Without Roy's help, Diamond Jim would be collecting on his own policy;" ironic, to say the least.

Hayden left town immediately. Molly said he was on his way to Madison, Wisconsin. He took all the t-shirt profits with him. I gave Molly the combination, and told her to check my mailbox at the student union. She did, but there were no fifty dollar bills to be found. My car was towed away—off the team, off the payroll.

A number of reporters, Ace Dunnigan being the most obnoxious of the bunch, came to the jail to interview me. I refused each and every one. I never really enjoyed doing press conferences after football games and I certainly wouldn't enjoy doing a post-riot wrap-up.

There were two more visitors. Marcus, who came the day after he was released from the hospital, limped in on crutches. He suffered a broken leg, a broken wrist, multiple lacerations, cracked ribs, and said his left ear wouldn't stop ringing. He couldn't thank me enough for what I did. His appreciation made it somewhat worthwhile. Marcus told me the NAACP hired an attorney and wanted to use him in a lawsuit against the city and the university. He hadn't made a decision on how, or if, he would proceed. I didn't offer an opinion on the matter.

The last visitor on the sign in sheet was my mother.

"Why, Tony, why did you throw your life away? Gaylord would have destroyed those two county prosecutors. All you had to do is say, 'Not guilty' and you wouldn't have had to spend a day in jail, much less go to prison. You threw away nineteen years of preparation to make you the best quarterback in the nation, the job every kid in America dreams of having."

Nice of you to drop by, Mom.

"Now we're going to have to wait three years to get you back in the game," she finishes her diatribe.

Sitting there, I knew I would never throw another pass, but I didn't tell her. What would be the point?

"Words cannot express my disappointment, Tony," she tells me. "I feel I have little left to live for in my life."

What a crock of bullshit. I don't verbalize, but this is the only thought that comes to my mind.

"How's Dad?" I ask.

"He's not any better, and he's not going to get any better."

"Tell him I love him."

---

The day I am scheduled to be transferred to the State Prison, my favorite guard watches me shower for the last time. As I am toweling off, he says, "You hear about Schwartz?

"The university president?" I ask.

200

"Yeah."

"What about him?"

"He drove his car into an on-coming log truck two days ago. He was crushed so bad, they might have to bury him inside the car." The guard pauses. "And it's all your fault."

"Sell that crap someplace else, buddy. Anyone who commits suicide is the author of his own tragedy," I pause. "And quit leering at me, would you?"

Later that morning, I was bussed to the State Prison about an hour away, to begin serving my sentence. I would arrive in time for the Christmas holidays. Joyous Noel.

Jail, compared to prison, is a vacation. Prison is past horrible. The filth, the food, the boredom, the absolute worthlessness of the situation is past unimaginable. Locking a person up in an 8 x 10 space, eighteen hours a day, seven days a week is hardly *rehabilitation*.

They threw me in with the worst of the worst; murderers, muggers, thieves, drug dealers. The idea of making Touchdown Tony an example of what happens to you if you're caught protesting against the machine, was definitely the game plan. Except for solitary confinement, they would have had a hard time making my hard time, harder. I was frightened out of my mind. I was afraid to breathe. You name the crime, and one of the guys around me would brag about it. In my first week I witnessed two stabbings, three fights, and four inmates being beaten senselessly by the guards. I stayed in my cell as many hours as I could. My roommate was Charley, a lifer, convicted of two assaults and two murders, but six years into his eighty-year sentence, he found the Lord. Charley was kind enough to teach me the do's and don'ts of prison life. His lessons were vital to my survival. In exchange, I taught him how to read.

Molly visited every Sunday. She found herself a job as a waitress at a truck stop, and rented Jerry's bedroom from Ruthie—a certain amount of irony there too. "We're in a race, Tony," she said. "Who will be first, me to graduate from high school, or you to be released from prison?"

"I hope you graduate soon," I tell her. "But, God, I hope I win."

Each Sunday, when the bell rang to end visitation, I'd watch her walk away, and my heart would break. Sometimes, all that kept me going was waiting for the next Sunday, when she would return to visit.

After six months, I was transferred to a minimum-security section of the facility. I taught physical education to the inmates, played on the softball team, and would handicap the upcoming college games so the guards could make more informed bets. I won a heck of a lot more than I lost. I read hundreds of books, including every word Shakespeare ever wrote. I wrote letters to Molly, Dad, Marcus, even Ralph and Ernie. I learned to play chess. I studied topics I was supposed to study in college. I learned a lot about a lot of things, but a lot more about myself. I did sit-ups and push-ups, not only to keep in shape, but also to expend the pent-up energy inside me. Some of my days went by quickly, but most lasted, what seemed to be, forever.

Mom visited once.

"Your father died," she said almost in a matter of fact tone. "They said it was Dementia-related Amyotrophic Lateral Sclerosis."

"What's that?"

"What difference does it make?" she snaps back at me. "He's gone."

I decided I'd cry later. "Did you read him my letters?"

"Yes."

The way she replied, I knew she was lying.

"What are you going to do, Mother?"

"Why would you care?"

"Because you're my mother."

"Everything I've ever lived for is either in prison or dead," she tells me. "So, I don't see myself with a lot of choices, Tony."

I don't respond. What would be the point?

Again, Mom, thanks for stopping by.

---

My release from prison came six months early. I spent 548 days incarcerated. They were the worst days of my life.

The times and tempers of the nation had changed in the months I spent behind bars. The press seldom wrote or spoke of the war as being right or wrong. It only discussed how and when America would get out. Not one news reporter came to my release, not even Ace Dunnigan, which was fine with me.

It was cold and rainy the day I became a free man. Molly met me outside the gate and as I held her in my arms more of my tears fell than raindrops from the sky. With her in my arms, wrapped as tight as a birthday present's bow, I felt as If I had won the ultimate prize, in the biggest game, in the grandest arena, life had to offer.

We moved halfway across the country to a city where few, if anyone, knew the name, Touchdown Tony McIntyre. I started going by the name Anthony, just to be sure. My first job was collecting trash. I washed dishes, mopped floors, cleaned toilets; and those were some of my better employments. I went back to school, not a big university, but to a community college. While in prison, I became fascinated with the workings of the human body, and started taking classes to become a physical therapist.

Our first apartment was a one-room studio. We had a mattress, table and two chairs, a radio, but no TV. We ate soup or spaghetti most nights, tea and toast most days. To others it would have been a depressing, awful life. I loved it. After eighteen months in a prison cell, the studio apartment was a small slice of heaven. We laughed, loved, talked of our future, and dreamed of what could be. In a year, we moved up to a two-room place. We needed more space, since a baby was on the way. We were thrilled, excited, and happy beyond belief. The day my first daughter was born was the second happiest day of my life.

It took me five years of night school, part time jobs, sleepless nights, cold cereal, and bus rides, but I received my certification to practice physical therapy. I looked for a job, but no one wanted a therapist with a criminal record. So, I hung out my own shingle. It was tough at first; I had to keep working as a short order cook to pay the bills at home, but one by one, the patients came through the door. I turned no one away. If they couldn't afford treatment, I'd barter. One guy paid me with a live pig. I took cases my competition refused. Some were so bruised, beaten, battered, and broken, there was little hope for recovery; some weren't even that lucky. I treated one high school boy, who took a vicious hit running an inside curl route, and couldn't get up from the turf. It took six months of hard, grueling work for him to walk again. Word spread of his recovery, and I started seeing injured kids from Pop Warner all the way to NCAA Division One. I did my best to help each and every one of them.

We moved to a suburb of a big city. My practice grew. I never stop learning. I am recognized as an expert in the treatment of patients with ALS, Lou Gehrig's disease. We bought our first house when I was thirty-seven years old. I volunteer my services at the county jail one night a week.

I've done okay. I'm considered successful—won a few accolades, got a few awards. But I am most proud of the fact that in all the years I have never once forgotten, or stopped working, to keep my three daughters and loving wife number one on my priority list.

Mom passed away in 1981. She was alone when she died.

EPILOG

I missed the luncheon.

"Where have you been?" Ellen, my middle daughter, asks, as I meet the family on their way out of the student union. "The president mentioned you twice and all anyone saw was an empty chair."

Molly laughs; she knows.

"I was out visiting a guy I used to know."

"Is Marcus here?" Mary asks.

"No, he said he's booked this weekend."

Marcus became somewhat of a celebrity. If you watch PBS Specials on Black History, Voting Rights, or the Civil Rights Movement, Professor Marcus Jones is always one of the talking heads in the story. Good for you, my friend.

"Another guy in a wheelchair, who talked funny, came by looking for you, Dad," Ellen says.

Steve Carlton.

I heard through a very long grapevine that Steve and Cindy never married. She ended up taking care of her father and subsequently took over the family business, "If it's insurance you need, see Cindy Bradley." Steve went to Vietnam, was wounded in the line of duty from what was listed as *friendly fire*. Paralyzed from the waist down, he has managed the American Legion Hall for over thirty years.

Praytel did get his shot in the NFL. He was the Offensive Coordinator for the Rams the year they went one-and-thirteen.

Arthur is a Minister in Pasadena, California.

Ralph and Ernie own thirty-seven Taco Bell restaurants.

General August Brown was convicted of taking bribes for entry into the National Guard, and did time in the same prison as I. Small world.

Swallow Lumber went belly up during the housing slump in the late seventies. Eugene's wife took him to the cleaners in their divorce.

Hayden made a fortune in the telemarketing business.

Ace Dunnigan was punched in the mouth interviewing an angry tight end. He developed a bad lisp, and left the airways.

"Our will and fates do so contrary run." William Shakespeare.

---

President Randall Alton, president of the Pioneer Athletic Association, stands on the outdoor stage of the student union, which hasn't changed all that much in almost forty years. He addresses the assembled, "We are here today to set into stone, a man far overdue to be honored for his achievements. Iron Mike McIntyre was the first man to be named an All American from this University. He was the first player to be chosen in the NFL draft of 1949. Iron Mike was a player to be admired. He was the consummate competitor, never afraid of a challenge. He put his heart, mind, body, and soul on the line, every down he played. No man hit harder, worked harder, or tried to win, more than Iron Mike McIntyre." Randall pauses. "I would like to invite Mike's son, Touchdown Tony McIntyre, to join me on the stage for the unveiling of the award.

I haven't heard that name in a lot of years, and can't say I miss it.

There is applause from the one hundred or so people in the audience. The most noise comes from my family. I walk up slowly, and position myself at the corner of the building.

"Tony, would you please do the honors."

I lift a red sheet from the square pillar, revealing a shiny, brass plaque embedded in the cornerstone. Dad's picture, name, dates, and a list of his football accomplishments are displayed.

"Tony, would you like to say a few words?"

I don't, but I will.

I walk slowly behind the podium.

"My Dad would appreciate this honor. If he were here today,

he would thank Mr. Alton, University President Webb, the Pioneer Athletic Association, and his fellow teammates. Dad is no longer with us. Please allow me to thank all of you for him.

"My father was a great football player, but for those who only knew him on the field, let me tell you my father was a much greater man off the field. My dad taught me resilience, pride, sacrifice, determination, what it meant to be the best, and how to overcome the harshest of life's injustices. He never complained, blamed another, or possessed an ounce of self-pity. He taught me in actions, in words, and when he could no longer speak or move, he taught me by example. Some have said Dad got a rotten deal and was literally cut down in the prime of his life. I disagree. My father faced adversity and disaster, the same way he faced an opposing lineman, with a fierce determination and force. My dad never backed down from a challenge, never stayed down after being hurt, and never gave up hope, even when the clock was running out.

"The most important lesson my father instilled into me was to think for myself, to come to my own conclusions on what is right and what is wrong. And, most importantly, never to hesitate to act on my beliefs, no matter what the consequences may be.

"I stand before you today, and can honestly say, no matter what I do, what I've done, and what I ever will become, I will never be more than my father's son."

There is a smattering of applause as I walk slowly back across the stage, down the steps to my waiting family. They all wear smiles of pride. Molly takes me by the arm, pulls me down to her, and whispers into my ear. "You did good. I've never been so proud of my husband."

The End

AUTHOR'S NOTE

Hell No, We Won't Go is a work of fiction, but almost every event in this story did actually take place. The events did not occur on the same campus, or during the same year, or to the same people, but they did happen. I was there, and in the middle of a lot of it. The characters in the story are people, or combinations of people, I knew, knew of, or came in contact with during my college years.

The 1960's were a turbulent time in America. Assassinations, protests, bombings, love-ins, riots, drugs, free love, free speech all blossomed and flourished.  The Sixties were also one hell of a lot of fun.

I have always felt fortunate to have grown up in such a phenomenal era.

Special thanks to fellow author Teresa Burrell for her legalese and writing expertise during the many months of this novel's creation.